I0637478

HUB CITY MENACE

JAQUILLE M. WHITE

LOCK DOWN PUBLICATIONS AND CA$H PRESENTS

Lock Down Publications

P.O. Box 944

Stockbridge, GA 30281

www.lockdownpublications.com

Like our page on Facebook: Lock Down Publications

www.facebook.com/lockdownpublications.ldp

STAY CONNECTED WITH US!

Text **LOCKDOWN** to 22828 to stay up-to-date with new releases, sneak peaks, contests and more...

Like our page on Facebook:
Lock Down Publications

Join Lock Down Publications/The New Era Reading Group

Visit our website:
www.lockdownpublications.com

Follow us on Instagram:
Lock Down Publications

Email Us: We want to hear from you!

ACKNOWLEDGMENTS

Well, first and foremost, I'd like to give the utmost praise and thanks to the man above. We all know without him nothings possible. If it weren't for his grace and glory, my life would be a whole 'nother story.

Secondly, I'd like to thank CEO Ca$h and the entire LDP staff who had a hand in making this book happen, and turning one of my dreams into reality. Ain't no feeling like this! Appreciate you guys for seeing my potential and giving me the opportunity to showcase my talents to the world!

I want to give a shout out to Texas...806... stand up!

Shout out to 'Playa Pat' Allen, CEO of "Playa Made Clothing" out of Odessa, Texas, 432! You came in the clutch on this. And I ain't even gotta say more. You a real one, bro. Y'all tap in wit em'!

Shout out to the select few who believed in me before this blew up... you know who you are!

To all my family & children... I love y'all!

We up!

And last but surely not least, RIP to my grandfather, Michael D. Price.

Lord knows!

DEDICATION

As the center of my life, the fuel and motivation to my many aspirations, I feel it's only appropriate that I dedicate this book to my two sons, Jayden and Jordan.
In the "oh-so-real" lyrics of Houston, Texas native and rapper, Lil KeKe, "I'm born and raised, but I ain't tryna die up in tha hood/I want my sons to know that daddy doin' something' good!"
To my young kings, "I love y'all! Place none above y'all! Remember, always be your Brother's Keeper."

AUTHOR'S NOTE
"URBAN FICTION"

My personal take on "Urban Fiction" is to write and create a believable story with imaginary characters and events, all through the lens and scope of a so-called "Street Perspective." While this particular genre may be deemed by some as exaggeration, ghetto, demoralizing or unrealistic, most of these stories are generally derived from both real events and people in some form of another. The shocking tales of a kingpin's crusades, broad day massacres, deep law enforcement corruption, mind blowing sexual trysts and hood-rat melodrama are only the tip of the iceberg.

The novels you read may very well be a product of the author's vivid imagination, but I believe behind every novel lies a sliver of truth. The ideas, plots and undertones didn't just sprout from thin air. "Urban Fiction" is the life we live, some of us more than others. Open your eyes and minds and surely you'll see...

1

PROLOGUE

ONE COLD AND RAINY NIGHT, deep within the ghettos of a West Texas hood, an unforeseen tragedy struck in the basement of a dilapidated, two-story home. The rugged structure was sandwiched in between two equally tattered homes, tucked away at the end of a secluded cul-de-sac, on a block the locals dubbed "Dead Street."

Lurking in the darkness of a heavily brewing thunderstorm this night, was a man named Jax. He was heading in the direction of the house in the middle of the cul-de-sac, waiting patiently for the right time to make his move. Before he took steps he couldn't retract, he scoped the area and unconsciously thought about the colorful history of "Dead Street."

The house on the left of the cul-de-sac was rather decent looking when being compared to its neighbors. Before the feds had it boarded up and completely sealed off from public use, thus leaving it in its abandoned state since

'04, it was a booming trap house that belonged to a noto-rious street hustler named BIG D.

BIG D was in fact one of the most prolific drug lords of his era in the mid-90s to the early 2000s. In just a few years he'd acquired it all! Money, power, respect, fame in the street, you name it. At one point during his brief reign he felt untouchable and to tell the truth, he was.

Eventually though, it would be his own loose lips that sank the ship and led to his undoing.

Laid up one night 'pillow talkin'' with a beautiful woman named Vivian Anderson cost him everything he'd worked so hard for. BIG D had been fucking Vivian for months, slowly catching real feelings for her. He was doing his best to impress her and while doing so, he got way too comfortable. After one of their many wild sexual trysts, BIG D revealed some vital details of his day-to-day drug operations that eventually cost him his freedom.

The woman BIG D was falling for turned out to be an undercover DEA agent. True to her job, every bit of infor-mation she collected during their faux relationship, she used against him on the stand during his epic federal trial. As a result of overwhelming evidence, he'd been found guilty on all charges brought against him.

On the day of his sentencing, BIG D stood behind the defendant's table in court as a blinding rage overtook his body when the presiding judge sentenced him to serve LIFE without the possibility of parole. Judge Nancy Sullivan seemed to smile with such effortless smugness and delight when she slammed her gavel down with such finality.

The realization of his fate setting in, BIG D hung his

head low while grilling his diamond teeth. He cursed himself for slipping, then said a silent prayer for forgiveness for the crimes he was about to commit.

After being shackled at the ankles and having his wrists bound by solid steel cuffs in front of him due to his considerable girth, BIG D was escorted toward the side door of the courtroom where he'd be taken away... Forever! Taking slow steps, he looked around the room watching all the white faces around him gloat and openly bask in victory of another successful trial. To them, the power of taking another niggas life away was more satisfying than making a large sum of money. Ironically, that day many in the room were able to do both.

At this point, BIG D grew livid and was ready to even the score. He was stuck in stride between two tall well-built officers but wouldn't let that stop him. Taking a deep breath, he paused and gazed down at both of the officers' hips before promptly springing into action.

The officer on the left side of BIG D was a left-handed shooter, which meant his gun was out of reach. Luckily, the officer on his right was also a lefty, which gave him easy access to the deadly weapon.

Quickly snatching the firearm out its holster and disarming the safety, BIG D pulled the trigger within milliseconds, delivering two lethal headshots to his former escorts. Doing a hundred-eighty-degree spin, he discharged the weapon again, striking the two bailiffs at the rear end of the courtroom, who were completely off guard and ill prepared to handle someone of BIG D's caliber.

Shooting with the deadly precision of trained military operatives, BIG D had eliminated all four officers in attendance in rapid succession. Then and only then did a sense of calm come over him. Not because he was done though... He was far from done. It was just that he knew he had all three of the people he deemed truly responsible for the outcome of his life, right where he wanted them. And now nobody in the world could save them if he moved fast.

Hobbling over to the closest dead officer, BIG D reached down, fumbling through the officer's uniform pocket and searching for the key that would enable him to move more freely, for what he assumed would be the last few minutes of his life.

When the initial gunshots rang out in the courtroom, chaos ensued as people began to scream to the tops of their lungs, all while trying to escape the perceived danger, trampling over one another in a desperate attempt to flee. Scanning the panicked room, BIG D locked eyes with his first victim, who was hiding sheepishly behind the cover of the sturdy mahogany defendant's table.

The man's name was Carl Piper. He was sixty-one years old, balding on top and fairly overweight. Mr. Piper was a shady defense lawyer who hid behind a facade so well-crafted, you wouldn't notice until it was too late. This time though, he made the mistake of selling out the wrong client.

"Mr. Cook, please think about what you are doing," the lawyer pleaded as he tried to back away from his attacker. He, as well as the other two soon-to-be victims were scared shitless of the six foot three, three-hundred-fifty-pound man the mean streets called BIG D.

Reaching down under the table with a mammoth sized hand, BIG D grabbed Mr. Piper by the throat and kneed the man with such tremendous force, the aging fellow lost control of his bladder.

"Muthafucka, you lied to me! I gave you two-hundred-fifty-thousand stacks! A quarter-million fuckin' dollars! You gave me your word that if we denied the plea and proceeded with trial, you could get me off!" BIG D roared with anger.

The cat had Mr. Piper's tongue. BIG D gave his most serious look and raised the gun to the lawyer's head. "You played me," he said harshly.

Mr. Piper stood there trembling in silence and soaking in his own urine. "What do you have to say for yourself?" BIG D asked, pressing the gun into the lawyer's eye socket.

"Mr. Cook, be-believe me when I say that I tried —" The loud boom of the gun echoed through the almost empty courtroom as BIG D ended the lawyer's lie and life simultaneously.

The federal judge, Nancy Sullivan sat on the bench of the 364th District Court for over twenty-five years, over-sentencing every nigga she could. In ninety-nine percent of the cases she tried that resulted in life sentences being issued, or a number of years so high it could be equated to life, minorities were the unfortunate recipients. The occasional cases she tried involving those of less color usually resulted in the defendant walking out of her courtroom with a slap on their wrist and smiles on their faces.

For years, Judge Sullivan ran this courtroom with an iron first, but now she sat atop the room in her plush swivel chair, frozen solid with the kind of fear only karma could bring as she laid witness to the homicidal massacre occurring.

Everyone knew the facts about Judge Sullivan. But in the cold world we live in, her superiors often agreed or simply turned a blind eye to her misguided sense of justice. On this day though, BIG D made sure her racist ass would never take the life away of any more black or brown people.

BIG D approached the bench where she sat, wearing a menacing scowl on his face that sent shockwaves of terror through her old bones. Judge Sullivan knew then her time had come but before she would be removed from this world, she had a few parting words for Mr. Cook.

"Fuck you, nigger! I hope your black ass burns in the fiery pits of hell," she spat angrily as her stale green eyes pierced into BIG D.

He replied, "You sentenced me to life, so now... I'm going to sentence you to death. Oh yeah, as far as hell goes... I guess I'll see you there, bitch!" And at that moment, he let five rounds go from the pistol, putting four bullets in her flowing black gown and one slug in her throat, stopping the constant beat of her icy heart.

Still holding the smoking gun, BIG D checked the magazine and revealed it held six more lead tickets of death, more than enough to finish what he started.

Vivian was beyond terrified as she silently crouched behind the panel of the witness stand. She cried tears the size of rain drops, while saying prayers to a God that would never answer that day. Vivian had hurt BIG D more than anyone ever had and now she was going to pay for it.

A full month prior to one of the most high-profile trials in Texas, Vivian Anderson stepped into a private clinic just some thirty miles away from town in a neighboring city.

Wearing a pair of Chanel sunglasses that hid her entire face, she moved cautiously, watching her surroundings in fear of being spotted.

A sexy receptionist named Tina took down Ms. Anderson's information after she arrived and told her to have a seat in the waiting area. Not long after, Dr. Thomas called Vivian back to his office to start on the pre-scheduled appointment.

The moment Vivian left the doctor's office, she felt extremely weak and very sore. That day, she had made a painful decision, a decision that doomed her soul and sealed her fate. Vivian planned on taking this secret to her grave but Tina, the receptionist, saw it differently. The information she'd just come across was her golden ticket back into BIG D's good graces.

A week before BIG D's sentencing, he was called out of his cell for a surprise visit. Tina sat there in the visitation booth looking good as ever! Her hair, nails, make-up and everything was on fleek. The tight outfit hugging her frame made her look goddess-like, but BIG D didn't give a fuck about that. His life was on the line so he definitely didn't have time for Tina's scandalous ass.

"What the fuck do you want?" BIG D snarled through the phone.

In a sweet and tender voice, Tina said, "Calm down, baby, I just came to see how you were holding up. "

"Ha! Bitch, you must done lost yo' rabbit ass mind. You know damn well I don't fuck with you like that," BIG D stated dryly before attempting to hang the phone up and leave the booth.

"Daddy! Wait! I got some news you can use... you

need to hear this!" Tina pushed out. Something about the sincerity in her voice made him stay put and hear her out.

"What the fuck is it?" D hissed.

"Look, D." Tina wiped her moist eyes. "I miss you so much," she stressed, "but I'm only going to give you this info if you promise to give me another chance." Tina was dead serious as the tears rolled in constant rhythm down her caramel-complexioned cheeks.

BIG D sat there in silence, weighing the decision in his mind for quite some time before reluctantly agreeing to her terms, even though he had no intentions of really honoring the promise.

What Tina revealed to BIG D in the visitation booth that day broke him down. That dreaded info was ultimately what made him lose his shit in the courtroom.

"Hhhh!" Vivian shrieked in pain, as BIG D landed a viscous blow directly to her head with the business end of the hot pistol in his hand.

"Shut up, bitch! You thought I wouldn't find out, huh! Huh?" BIG D roared, while landing more crushing blows to the woman's mid-section with his heavy foot.

Vivian was in a world of pain that was only going to get worse. "What are you talking about?" she managed to say, wiping blood from her mouth. She had a very eerie feeling he knew exactly what she'd done, because of the pain lingering in his voice and the welled-up tears in the corners of his eyelids. Still though, she played dumb.

Boom! A thunderous shot rang out and struck her in the lower left torso. "Tell me why, Viv. Why would you kill my only child?" BIG D demanded to know.

Vivian's eyes grew wide with fear as the truth spewed

from BIG D's lips. She wasn't stupid, she knew she'd fucked up big time. And without any doubt, she was going to die.

"D, listen. It was never supposed to go this far. I never intended for you to catch feelings. I had no choice but to abort the baby. I was only doing my job," Vivian admitted, just as D struck with another brutal blow.

"You were just doing your fuckin' job, huh?" BIG D asked, sarcasm dripping from every word. "Well, don't mind me for doin' mine!"

Then he pulled the trigger again, striking the woman in the abdomen once more. Vivian laid there on the court-room floor, drowning in a burgundy pool of her own blood from the two burning gunshot wounds in her gut. BIG D stepped over Vivian, pointing the gun down at her head. With hate fueling his every move, he said, "Any last words, bitch?"

"I'm sorry…" Vivian mumbled in a rasp.

Then without further ado, BIG D sent Vivian Anderson to the afterlife, pumping four lead slugs into the woman's beautiful face.

As his murderous rage boiled over and subsided completely, BIG D snapped back to reality and realized it was time to face the music. During the chaos, an entire SWAT team surrounded the courtroom with specific orders to take down the hostile inside, using deadly force. What SWAT didn't know was that their target was something more than some simple-minded men could understand or gather. BIG D by far was no ordinary man.

He was extraordinary in fact and above all, he was hard to kill. This was the story spread around the hood about the house on the left. To all who heard it, BIG D was an urban legend.

————

The charred and barely standing house on the right had a much different vibe and back-story than its neighbor. According to the hood about ten years back, shortly before the end of BIG D's reign, a wife and mother of three named Sharon came home early from work after a long day. Sharon was looking to relax a bit before getting dinner ready for her family.

However, Sharon was not in any way prepared to be again devastated by the one and only man she'd ever loved.

Not expecting his wife's early arrival, Andre Carter was in the bedroom he shared with his wife, getting some of the best head ever from a real curvaceous woman he met in the neighborhood and secretly had his eyes on. All while his three small children Terrence, Terry, and Tory played in the backyard. Sharon had told Andre earlier that day that she'd be working late again, and true enough, she was going to be until her dear friend Mecia offered to cover the rest of her shift. So, Sharon decided to pop-up without a warning so she could surprise her loving children and husband of a decade.

Pulling up to the house, she couldn't help but notice a familiar-looking white Benz sitting in the driveway. Sharon shrugged, putting it off, incorrectly assuming the car belonged to one of Andre's homeboys. She parked behind the car and went inside her home. As she waltzed through the door, she kicked off her shoes and stretched her overly worked body. Something immediately seemed off about the overall vibe of the house. It was way too quiet. And with three bad ass kids, silence was rare. In search of her babies, Sharon walked through the house, only to find them all in the backyard giggling away.

With no distractions, dinner could be all ready within the hour so she let the children be. Plus, Sharon figured maybe she could spend a few adult minutes with Andre once he got rid of his friend.

Sharon opened the door to the basement, but found it dark, dank and empty. Anytime Andre had company, this was where they hung out smoking, drinking, and shooting the shit. In a flash, mixed emotions overcame Sharon as she shot up the stairs to her master bedroom quickly yet quietly. Slowly, she twisted the doorknob, cracking the view in about two inches.

The visuals of Andre's infidelity sickened Sharon, but positively confirmed her suspicions, causing her heart to ice-over.

Andre was now plowing inside of some woman in their bed with reckless abandon, like he was a single man, and his sons and daughter weren't just feet away outside. Angry enough to kill, Sharon set out her plan of diabolical revenge. She closed the door just as quietly as she opened it, then flew down the staircase.

Once Sharon gathered her children, she packed them all into the back seat of the car, doing her best to avoid the many questions they asked. The slightest bit of guilt came into Sharon's mind knowing she was about to do harm to the father of her children.

Leaving the kids in the car for just a second, Sharon

entered the garage and found exactly what she was looking for. She poured a trail of highly flammable gasoline from the master bedroom all the way to the front and back porches, then sporadically through the rest of the home.

She picked up a pack of Andre's Newport cigarettes and Bic lighter off the coffee table, lit the square and smoked it down to the green lined filter. In her mind she kept saying, *Enough is enough*!

Stepping outside on the porch, cigarette butt in hand, heartbroken, Sharon managed to smirk a little bit thinking of the irony of her current situation. Over her ten-year marriage to Andre Carter, he brought home two STDs, burning Sharon in the process. In the end, Sharon made sure to burn him back. On that day, Sharon had officially lost all trust and love for men. Even for her two sons who reminded her of their father constantly. From the second the flames sparked on those fresh pools of gas... the Carter family would never be the same.

Now, as for the house in the middle, it was standing on its last limb and wasn't the easiest on the eyes, but for all its lack in luster, this was still the place in the hood where everyone wanted to be in search of a good time.

The old, decrepit house was nicknamed "Tha Spot." Everyone called it Tha Spot because no matter what your vice was, be it drugs, violence, gambling or sex, this place offered the opportunity for you to get your fix. Each floor of Tha Spot was different and designed to cater to a specific vice.

On the main floor, consisting of the living room, guest room, kitchen and bathroom is where all the hood parties and kickbacks took place on birthdays, holidays or really any day. If alcohol or any drug was your vice, that was the space you'd more than likely help occupy. The three bedrooms upstairs were always reserved by the pimps and the slew of hoes they had turning tricks. If you weren't into buying or selling pussy, you were surely on the wrong floor. Out in the backyard on weekends, a legendary street fighter named Night-Night ran cards of bare-knuckle fights that usually turned a large crowd, but lately the fight scene had been put on hold after a fighter named K.O. died in a match.

Down below in the basement is where all the real action took place. In this spacious area dedicated to the real gamblers awaited tables for every game street niggas, like to wager some money on poker, pool, dominoes, spades, and dice.

Two seventy-inch LED plasma TVs lined the decaying walls in the corner, right in front of a dusty old sofa. One TV was for video game bets or the occasional "flick" and the other TV was set up to watch NFL or NBA games, or other events like fights or music award shows.

On any given day more money changed hands and was circulated down there than in a local bank. To many in the hood, Tha Spot was just a lil get away. Somewhere to go and pass time. But for Jax, this was his second home.

PART I

STARTED FROM THE BOTTOM

1

BLOOD ON THE WALLS

AFTER LEAVING Tha Spot just a few minutes ago, Jax finally made it to his car parked at the end of the block. Approaching the driver's side door, he hit the unlock button on his electronic key fob and hastily jumped in the whip, trying to dodge the falling rain.

In a rush, he dug into the glovebox for a second, throwing around registration papers and old receipts until he found the O.G. Kush blunt he'd rolled earlier, hit a few times then abandoned. To Jax, blowin' on some grade-A while sittin' behind the wheel of his '84 box Chevy Caprice is where he did some of his best thinkin'. And some thinkin' he really needed to do.

Sparking a warm orange flame to the blunt, Jax tilted back and relaxed further into his seat as he savored the flavor and potency of the Kush with each sharp inhale. Upon slow rhythmic exhales, the sweet, toxic smoke invaded the confined space around him, lingering in thick transparent clouds thus elevating his cerebral high.

Normally, Jax was a very cool, calm and collected guy, but the prior events that transpired in Tha Spot about half an hour ago suddenly changed his usual demeanor and had him on edge.

Just before the private smoke session he was currently engaging in, Jax was down in the basement of Tha Spot, shooting dice with two niggas named T.C. and Lil Dave, while two other niggas named Cali and Show stood by and watched all the action take place.

Jax went up in Tha Spot with two bandz on 'im and expected to come out with about four bandz or better as usual. To say he was shocked or somewhat sour when he left out that bitch with nothing would be a complete under-statement.

Now this was a very rare and unusual situation for Jax because he always won! Winning was embedded in his DNA. No matter what the game was, be it poker, dice, video games or even betting on some random sports event, he alway seemed to have some sort of supernatural advan-tage over his opponents and manage to reign victorious.

The many people who witnessed this phenomenon with their own eyes still couldn't seem to understand how it was possible how the odds always seemed to fall in his favor. Nobody was perfect and there were always way too many eyes and ears around Tha Spot for someone to cheat. So Jax's unexplainable luck baffled all who bet their dollar to his.

Jax believed the reason he was able to win at every-thing, time and time again, was because of all the good he did with his earnings. See, his mother Mecia had fallen very ill over the years. So much so she could no longer support the family of five on her own. As her health depleted, so did her funds she made as a nurse at the local hospital.

With neither of her children's fathers in the picture, and her older brother spending his life in prison, Mecia called on her oldest son, Jax to help carry the load life pushed down on her shoulders.

Rightfully so, Jax stepped up and was doing the best he could to help take care of bills and other things around the house. Just three short years out of high school though, and already having a son of his own to raise, his plate was full to say the least. So every dollar counted and was much needed. He had no room for losses.

As he reached the blissful ends of his O.G., he felt the soothing effects of the THC bring his temper down a notch, but his mind was still set on what he planned to do.

Calmly, Jax got out the shelter of his car and paced around to the trunk as a constant drum of raindrops drizzled down from above, pelting the crown of his dark hoodie.

He opened the trunk with his fob and reached down inside, placing his right thumb on a blue-lit, LED biometric scanner concealed on the head of one of the many speakers. As the light went green, a six-digit code was requested on a small screen revealing itself on the adjacent speaker.

After a second to validate, a secret compartment began to unfold before his eyes and out popped the safe where he kept all his guns, drugs, and illegal narcotics. This genius of a contraption saved him from numerous felonies on countless occasions. The safe was so official, Jesus himself couldn't open it without Jax's thumb and code.

Without hesitation, Jax pulled out a custom, all-black

9mm semi-automatic handgun. On the side it read, "THE REAPER" and was upgraded with a disorienting strobe light, green-laser beam, thirty-round extended magazine and a six-inch silencer. In short, it was a bad muthafucker!

As Jax admired the gun's beauty, a bright bolt of lightning, followed by loud bursts of thunder rang out in the night as if right at that very moment, God was sending Jax a fair warning.

At first, Jax thought about just accepting the loss and going home, but something deep inside just wouldn't let him. Visions of mere payback clouded his brain as he took off in the direction of Tha Spot in pursuit of his loot.

Jax wasn't a psycho or a stone-cold killer by any means, but when provoked or done foul, he could be extremely dangerous. The way T.C. and Lil Dave did him, cappin' on 'im and leaving him high and dry, only added fuel to the fire burning within him. He was hot because any time he won and beat them niggas out of all they money, he'd always give some back because that's how he showed his respect and appreciation of the gamble. Plus, he knew early on that a broke man is dangerous and unpredictable. Jax was very humble and fair, so many respected him, but that night he was about to show a few young punks why they should fear him to

Stepping up on the porch of Tha Spot, Jax was greeted by GOAT for the second time that night. GOAT was an O.G. in tha hood and the official caretaker of Tha Spot, so everything that went down there went through him.

"Wassup youngsta, you back at it, huh?" GOAT asked in his deep, raspy voice.

"Yeah, O.G. Shit, I can't let them lil niggas have it like that. I gotta make somethin' shake," Jax replied.

"Aight, then." GOAT nodded his approval for entrance.

Due to the fact Jax had just been in Tha Spot about thirty minutes ago and GOAT was like an uncle to him, having known him since his early childhood days, he made the critical mistake of not searching him. As he gained access through the front door again, another deafening crash of lightning and thunder boomed through the crying skies.

Normally, Tha Spot was always packed to capacity at any time day or night, but the heavy thunderstorm cast over the city that night kept all the frequent visitors at bay. As Jax made his second trip to the basement, there were only nine souls present inside Tha Spot but he was only aware of eight, including his very own.

Three people wouldn't know what happened until it was too late. A man and two fine women were upstairs frolicking in each other's juices, oblivious to the turmoil stirring below. Four souls were about to perish at the hand of Jax. And one tortured soul would be witness to the unthinkable.

All of the targets were gathered around a tall table sharing deep laughs about the damage they'd done to Jax's pockets not long ago with some trick dice. As Jax crept silently down the wooden steps of the basement, he caught the ass end of a conversation between T.C. and Lil Dave that transformed his intentions from a simple robbery to something much more ill.

"Say my nigga, I don't know how you made that shit

work, but you really came through solid on that one," Lil Dave spoke as he thumbed through a pile of crisp twenties.

"I told you we was gone get that bitch ass nigga one day... Hahaha, he had me fucked up, thinkin' he was just gone hit me for three thousand last week then try to give me three hundred back like shit funny or somethin'... Man, fuck that nigga Jax. Far as I'm concerned, he got what he deserved, walkin' round' this bitch like he all that. Shit, when he comes back, I'ma bust his ass again with these janky muthafuckas. I got a lil brother to feed," T.C. boasted as he spared a look over his shoulder toward the TV section, then lightly rolled the loaded dice across the table top, hitting a seven.

"Man, where you get the bullshit ass dice anyway, fam?" Lil Dave questioned after he scooped up the dice and gave them a shake and roll himself.

"You remember my older cousin Tyreke, right?" T.C. asked.

"Yeah, I remember his square ass. Ha... what he got to do with those though?" Lil Dave capped.

"So he called me last night, lookin' to buy a zip. Said he was in town for a concert or something like that. Anyway, I pull up on 'im and he only got half the money and these," T.C. said, shaking the red-clear dice in his hand.

"Nigga, you sold that man some of that gas for a hundred and some damn dice?" Lil Dave scratched his head on that one.

T.C. looked at Dave with a smirk and said, "Check this out though. See, Tyreke got a job a few months back working doing security. He told me one night some burned-up, Freddy Kreuger lookin muthafucka named Dre came up in there and stung they ass for fifty Gs on the craps table, before the owner and Tyreke reviewed the security footage and seen how swiftly he switched their dice with these," T.C. explained. Then he showed all three men around the table how to roll the dice to hit your desired point every time and how to roll the occasional crap just to make the scam look good.

It was at that moment when Jax heard the real that everyone's fate was sealed.

"So... you muthafuckas thought y'all was just gone get down on a real one?" Jax shouted at them, popping up out of thin air, and catching them all by surprise. He had 'THE REAPER' raised eye level with each man at the table.

Deep down, each one of them knew they'd fucked up as they watched the devilish grin spread wide beneath the grizzly beard on Jax's golden face.

"Man... Jax, look... I-I didn't have shit to do with this. I don't even have no money!" Cali stated in a pathetic attempt to save his own ass. Jax's reputation preceded him outside of Tha Spot and Cali knew when the man in front of him raised his tool, he meant business.

Psht! A hollow tip barely whistled as it broke free of the matte black silencer and landed flush between Cali's eyes.

As his body fell lifelessly to the floor, Jax knew then he had crossed the path of no return. The rational side of his brain screamed, "Nigga, you trippin'!" but the much louder irrational side screamed, "Fuck these niggas! They don't care about you or what you're goin' through. They'd do the same to you if they could, so do 'em!" So in that moment, irrationality won.

"Jax, please don't kill me, man. I don't have any money either. All I did was watch. C'mon, man, we ain't ever had a problem before man, please!" Show begged.

"Yeah, I guess you're right... We ain't ever had no issues before. But, that changed earlier. You had full knowledge that your homeboys was trying some fraud ass shit and you just sat back and didn't say nun, just like that bum ass nigga Cali. Blame them!" Jax said, then squeezed two rounds in Show's chest.

T.C. and Lil Dave were completely silent, literally shaking in their Timberland boots.

Jax stepped closer to them, gun still aimed high and said with all seriousness, "Now for you two, where the fuck is my money?"

Simultaneously, Lil Dave and T.C. pointed to the table just off to the side of them where two thousand in cash lay beside the bogus dice.

"All of it!" Jax demanded, thrusting the gun suggestively.

"It's all there, man!" T.C. said.

Psht! Psht! THE REAPER expelled two more bullets, hitting T.C. and Lil Dave in the leg, causing them to collapse and cower in fear and agony.

"You muthafuckas still think I'm playin', run that shit!" Jax spat.

Following orders, T.C. and Lil Dave emptied their pockets and Jax quickly collected.

"Alright nigga, you got your money, mines, and you done popped two of my niggas," Lil Dave cried, "Let me go, think we are more than even." He stared at Jax, gritting his teeth and clenching his fresh leg wound.

"Okay, Lil Dave, I'ma let you go," Jax said with an air of sarcasm Lil Dave must not have caught.

Lil Dave managed to breathe a sigh of relief just before Jax stepped over him with THE REAPER pointed down and said, "Here you go... One-way ticket to the other side, muthafucka!" Psht! Psht! The 9mm sang as it claimed another body.

"Do you have anything to say, bitch-ass nigga?" Jax asked T.C. in a low growl.

T.C. just laid there in defeat, wincing in obvious pain. He never once made eye contact with Jax, his eyes stayed focused on the area around the couch in front of the two TV screens.

"You hear me, muthafucka?" Jax shouted as his damp Air Force One met T.C. 's rib cage.

Coughing blood, T.C. gained the strength to say his final words. "Fuck you, Jax! I know what I did was foul, but you ain't have to do all this. You ain't the only one that's tryna eat, my nigga... I got a family too!"

The 9mm went off four more times before T.C. could say more. He just laid there now, his dead eyes burning a hole in the couch as his soul rose and left his cooling body.

In Jax's mind, all he left behind that night was blood on the walls, but there was a soul THE REAPER did not put to rest. That minor slip-up would come back to haunt him forever.

Realizing the depth of what he'd done in that basement,

Jax knew in order to fully cover his tracks he'd have to end one more person as he made his escape from the bowels of Tha Spot.

GOAT… GOAT would be the only real witness for the bloodbath in the basement, so Jax felt he was doing the right thing when he snuck up behind him quietly and put two in his head, ending his life and his phone call.

As Jax discreetly pulled away from the secluded neighborhood in the wee hours of night, he couldn't help but realize the irony of the entire situation. The block nicknamed "Dead Street" was exactly that. The houses, the trees, the leaves, the hope and even the people were all dead! Or so he thought…

2

I'M WORRIED ABOUT YOUR SOUL

SUNDAY DINNERS at home with the family was one of the few things Jax actually looked forward to all week. After church service, Mecia would send him and his younger brother Marcus to the United Supermarket grocery store to buy food, while she and her two young daughters, Kam and Ke' would stay home, clean house and prepare to cook.

Nothing in the whole world was better than Mecia's home cooking. Especially after a week's worth of fast food eating, due to everyone's hectic schedules and various events. So normally everyone in the family absolutely couldn't wait for Sunday. This Sunday was even more special for Jax because he got to see his son Jr. and keep him for a few days.

Jax and Cori, Jr.'s mother, didn't seem to get along whatsoever. To Jax she was the epitome of childish, and she only allowed Jax to see his son when it was convenient for her. This sort of shit definitely didn't sit well with Jax, but there was only so much he could do about the situation. He was getting a lil bit of money, but most of it was spent on the family's meals, bills and necessities.

Cori knew the gravity of Jax's situation at home and how different things were for him since he went to jail a while back, but all in all, she didn't care. While he was in jail fighting his case, she filed for child support and sole custody, even though back in those days Jr. was just a newborn, and he was already giving her five hundred a month. Being incarcerated when the paperwork was originally filed, Jax was unable to attend the child support court and custody hearing to defend his rights as the child's father. As a result, he was stripped of all his parental rights to Jr., but was still ordered to pay child support at an increase of eight hundred a month.

So, with that situation being how it was, anytime he could get his son, he jumped at the opportunity no matter what was going on. After completing the grocery run, he scooped up Jr. and headed home.

While the women skillfully prepared dinner, Jax and Marcus were outside in the backyard going over Marcus' routes and plays, while Jr. babbled gibberish and happily played with his toys in the dirt.

Marcus was only twelve and still in middle school, but he was big for his age and really athletic. Hands down, he was one of the best football players in the city for his age group and showed tremendous promise of having a bright athletic future ahead. Jax, being the only male in Marcus' life, was hard on his little brother. He pushed him to be great because he too had an opportunity to excel in sports once, but when he was forced to grow up too soon and be a man, the mean streets took all his hopes of playing ball away. He simply refused to let the same happen to Marcus, what kind of brother would he be?

Ke' was the youngest sister. She was only thirteen and starting to come into womanhood. She was a sweet child, well mannered and behaved, rarely giving Mecia or anybody trouble.

Kam was the older of the two girls, she was sixteen going on sixty and a damn handful. She was a smart young girl with the singing voice of an angel, with the attitude of a little devil.

Though they were like night and day, the bond between the two sisters was inseparable, even through the normal childhood spats.

As dinner was complete and ready, Mecia called for everybody to gather around the table. She scooped up baby Jr. and held his little butt still in her lap, while she ordered everyone to close their eyes while she led them in prayer.

"Dear Heavenly Father," she called out to the man above, "Thank you so very much for this day. Another day none of us here were guaranteed. Thank you, oh Lord, for this food we are about to receive for the nourishment of our bodies and the fulfillment of our souls." she paused slightly and eyed Jax. His eyes remained shut. "I ask that you bless every person at this table and continue to show us all the way, Lord, Amen and Amen!" she concluded sincerely.

Plates were then passed and filled. Drinks poured to the brims of glasses until all around were satisfied.

"Well, y'all know the drill… who's going first?" Mecia asked, referring to the deal they had in place for Sunday dinners. It consisted of a time where all her children had the opportunity to speak up about the good and bad in their week.

"Um, my week was pretty good. School was school, nothing new there really… On another note though, me and the girls have been offered another gig this Saturday night at a spot downtown. Is it okay for me to go Ma, please?" Kam asked, praying Mecia said yes.

"You can go because I love the group. Baby, you girls do make some beautiful music. But listen to me clearly, if I find out you are up to no good, Kam… so help me God, I will put my —" Mecia was saying before a low snicker from Ke' cut her off.

"And just what are you laughing at, Lil Miss Thang?" Mecia asked sarcastically. She still bounced Jr. on a knee feeding him while maintaining her information probe.

"Nothing, Momma," Ke said flatly.

"Thought so," Mecia smiled. "So, how was your week with school and practice, baby girl?"

"School was good. I got an A-plus on Mrs. Suthers' math exam and dance practice went even better. I finally beat out Kimberly for the lead role in the next recital!" Ke said excitedly.

"That's great, baby. You know we'll all be there. I'm proud of you," Mecia said lovingly with a wink.

"Ma, I won player of the game again since I scored five touchdowns! And… Coach Johnson says I can go to the NFL," Marcus butted in, trying to edge and one up his big sisters.

"Well, look at you, you go, boy! Momma's proud of you too," Mecia said, shooting him a smile that soon twisted into a frown. "But I also got your new report card in the mail Friday and your grades are slipping again. I'm only going to say this once, fix it! Or there will be no NFL, no Xbox, TV or anything at all for you, mister!" she said sternly.

"Yes, Ma'am," Marcus said, then continued stuffing his face.

Now all attention went to Jax.

"How about you, son, any luck on a job yet?" Mecia asked, already knowing the answer.

Jax swallowed. "Not yet, Ma, but I do have a few interviews coming up soon. I'm sure something will pan out... if not, you know I'll figure something out to keep some money coming in. "

"That's what I'm afraid of, son, all money ain't good money. But you know that though, right?" Mecia said a little louder than she intended. Jr. jumped in her lap and turned to look at her wearily. She soothed him and in seconds he was picking at her plate again.

"May we be excused?" the three youngest asked in unison. They planned to leave the tension-filled room, go in the next room over and eavesdrop.

"Of course," Mecia said, retreating back to her sweet voice. "Clean y'all plates and drop them in the washer," she called over her shoulder.

"Okay, what's all this fuss about, Ma? Talk to me. I mean, for the last three or so years, I've been helpin' you make ends meet and you never once questioned how until recently, what's the issue?" Jax questioned curiously.

"Son, don't get me wrong, I appreciate all the help you have provided financially and physically with the kids, but I'm really worried about you." Mecia's eyes were sad.

"Ma, there's no need to be worried about me. I'm fine. Soon I'll get a good job and continue to help you out for as long as you need me to. I love you and them lil gremlins in there... we gone be okay," Jax said.

"Son, you're not listening to me. I'm worried about your soul. I've been hearing stories about you in those streets. I know you're no saint, but I don't need you to become a devil either!" Mecia spoke seriously.

Jax got up from the table and walked over to where his mother sat with Jr. He bent down and took them both into his arms, squeezing them slightly, trying to reassure her he was indeed okay and need not to worry. Mecia had a bad heart and Jax didn't want her to be in any more pain than what she already felt daily.

"Ma, I'm sorry if I've worried you or hurt you. I will do better, you have my word on that," Jax promised his mother.

"Thank you, son," she said and kissed his cheek. Then she began to clean Jr. and the mess he'd made. "Oh, yeah... Son, I need you to do me a favor," she said to Jax as he rose to his feet again.

Jax nodded.

"On Saturday, I need you to go visit your uncle. He's been asking about you and I think maybe if y'all have a heart-to-heart, you'll see the way life can go wrong if you don't change your ways."

"Okay, Ma, anything for you." And he turned to look at Jr. and said, "And anything for you too."

3

TEN BITCHES AND A BLACK BOOK

AFTER A LONG WEEK of running errands for his mother, getting his siblings to and from school and practices, Jax turned it in early on Friday night instead of heading over to Tha Spot as usual.

He figured it'd be for the best to let the heat die down a bit more. The hood was hot as fish grease after five dead bodies were found in a house that was supposed to be vacant. Plus, there were small rumbles being heard on the street about the police having a potential witness to the crime. Jax, of all people, knew that couldn't have been true. But even so, he'd rather be safe than sorry... and he had Jr. again, so why bother.

Saturday morning rolled around and Jax awoke to a beautiful sight. Jr. was playing with his face and smiling a brilliant smile trying to wake him and get his full attention. The moment was precious and cherished, for because of the current custodial situation with Cori, they didn't come as often as he liked.

It was just a bit past 7:00 am when he got out the bed and headed to the kitchen to make him and Jr. something to eat. They finished their meal and Jax played with his son for about an hour or so before he decided it was time to get ready for the day. He took Jr. to Kam and Ke's room so they could watch their nephew, while Jax went to go visit his uncle Derrick as requested by their mother.

Getting dressed, Jax threw on a comfortable Nike jumpsuit with his favorite pair of Air Max 95's. He hit his grill with Colgate and brushed down his spinnin' 360 waves to perfection. He added a few sprays of smell good and he was ready to go.

Derrick was housed in a federal prison about an hour outside the city, so Jax got in his Chevy, turned up the beats as high as the system allowed and hit the gas. Sixty-five minutes and a whole *Future* album later, Jax turned real slow and cut his bass down as he entered the barbed wire fencing of the prison facility.

Jax had been to the Lubbock County Jail before, so he had an idea of what to expect but in all actuality, what he was seeing was indeed quite different. The facility was huge and looked to be way nicer than the ones often shown on TV. Eventually, Jax found a parking spot but the walk seemed to be an hour away from the visitors' entrance.

Stepping through the glass doors labeled VISITATION in bold letters, Jax was greeted by a tall stocky guard in a dull gray uniform, wearing gloves and holding a metal detecting wand.

"Good morning, sir. If you would please step up, take

everything out of your pockets and place the items in the bucket in front of you," the guard ordered.

Jax followed the simple directions placing his keys, cell phone, and wallet in the designated bin.

"Step through the body scanner and wait to be patted down by the next officer," came further orders from Stocky.

When Jax passed the full inspection, he grabbed his belongings and took his place in line at the visitation registration window. Once he made it to the counter, an old lady with an unusually deep voice asked to see his identification and whom he was there to see.

"Derrick Cook," Jax answered, handing over his ID to the woman.

"Have a seat, sir, and you will be called out momentarily," she replied in a low octave.

While waiting, Jax began to feel a little nervous, truly not knowing what to expect of this visit. Overall, he had a cool relationship with his uncle who often wrote letters to the house, sent the family holiday cards and called occasionally but outside of that, he realized he really didn't quite know Derrick.

Ten minutes later, a door opened and a chubby lady waddled out. "Visitor for Cook," she squeaked.

Jax got up and followed her down a long hallway, leading him to a large reception area filled with lots of tables and a variety of fully stocked vending machines. They reached a desk where another officer sat and the chubby lady said, "Ms. Rios here will give you your seating arrangement. Have a good visit. " Then she turned on her heels and waddled off the way she came.

"A. Rios," Jax read the name tag on the woman's chest. He drank in the woman's natural beauty. She looked to be of some mixed race, definitely with black somewhere in the mix, but Jax had to admit the lady in front of him, perhaps in her mid-thirties was absolutely fine as hell!

"Table thirteen," she said to him, offering a gorgeous smile.

Jax pushed aside the thoughts tumbling through his head and proceeded on to the suggested table. As he made his way over, he looked around the packed room glancing at all of the other inmates engaging in their visits.

People from all walks of life filled the room carrying on in conversation, trading laughs, smiles, and eating food. Majority of the men there seemed rather calm and comfortable than what's normally portrayed of men in prison.

Not long after sitting down at the table, Jax turned in his seat when he heard a metal door at the back of the visitation room buzz open. In stepped an exceptionally large man who seemed to suck the air out of the room as he strode in Jax's direction. The man had to be at least sixfoot something and tip the scales at well over three hundred pounds. He stepped with confidence and a sense of power anyone could pick up on.

Some inmates saluted him as he passed out of love and respect. Others ducked and avoided eye contact out of weakness and fear.

To Jax's utter surprise the man stopped directly at his table, gazed down upon him and smiled a dazzling smile as the light within the room retracted beautifully off his diamond encrusted teeth.

"What's craccin', Nephew? Long time no see."

A confused look painted Jax's face in response to the man's statement he now concluded was his uncle Derrick. Jax remembered having phone convos and corresponding with him through letters as far back as middle school, but he didn't recall ever meeting the man in person.

Derrick picked up on the confused look on his oldest nephew's face and offered an explanation as he sat down. "Yeah, it's been a while... 'bout sixteen years now. "

"Damn, Unc, you been up in here for sixteen years?" Jax questioned, mind blown.

"Nah neph, I've only been incarcerated here for 'bout nine long years now. Seven years prior to that, I wasn't allowed to see y'all since you were just five... me and your mother weren't on the best of terms back then." Before Jax could even ask why, Derrick said, "How's everyone doing?"

"Well everyone is actually doing okay. Kam is still singing. She's the leader of this all girl group called 3BG and they have been making quite a name for themselves around the city. As for Ke, she is doing great in school like always. Honor-roll every month and she really has stepped it up with her dancing and ballet. She's supposed to have the lead role in some big recital coming up. Marcus has been on his best shit too, the kid is gettin' big and can really play some ball, Unc! Now I ain't sayin' he better than me or anything like that... but if he keeps it up, he will most definitely get a division 1 scholarship out of high school. He just needs to get his grades up."

Derrick smiled and nodded approvingly.

"I've been a'ight. I ain't gone lie tho', shit been kinda rough over the years trying to stay out of trouble, take care of my son Jr. and help Moms out with the youngins all at the same time… Plus, money been a lil funny, especially with Ma's work situation. Somehow I been makin' it work though," Jax revealed.

"Man, I'm sure glad to hear all the lil ones doing well. Nephew, I want to say I really appreciate all the help you're giving my sister. You know, sometimes as men we gotta do shit to take care of our families that most folks won't understand or condone. "

"Shit… I'm glad you see it that way cause Mom's really been on my ass lately, even though I'm the one keepin' the lights on. "

"How so?" Derrick asked.

"Well, lately she just been trippin' 'bout me not having an actual job and shit. Steady questioning how I'm making my money and all that, how I'm spending my free time… She claim she been hearing stories 'bout me, but I don't see how she could. You know Ma ain't in the streets like that. "

"Nephew, I'ma tell you right now she don't have to be in the streets 'like that,' the streets talk. I've been here damn near a decade and I've known damn near your every move since you 'jumped off tha' porch.' So, I can only imagine what a mother like yours has come to learn of her oldest child," Derrick stated.

A look of shock crossed Jax's face. He'd always considered himself to be a smooth operator, but listening to what his uncle was saying, he was second guessing his stealth. "How could you possibly know what's going on outside these walls?" Jax challenged, raising an eyebrow.

"Back in my era, I was somebody... No, scratch that shit, I still am somebody. I got eyes and ears everywhere, Neph. As a matter of fact, you unknowingly cross paths with one of my main men at least once a week... But all that's conversation for next time. Today is all about you, Jax."

"What about me, Unc?"

"I know all about Mecia's heart issue and the surgery the doctors suggested she have about three years ago. I know how much of a bind you guys have been in trying to save the money up. And I know about that situation that took place when you were in school, and you and your friends went to jail trying to get the money. I know all too well how hard shit has been, so now I'm here to offer a helping hand," he said with sincerity.

With an untamed attitude, Jax said, "A helping hand? Nigga where the fuck you been, huh? Why would you try to offer your muthafuckin' help, now that it's too late? Why not help from the fuckin' beginning if you knew?"

Derrick understood Jax's anger and he was entitled to it. Calmly, he said, "Like I told you before, me and your mother weren't on the best of terms. I tried to help time and time again, but she would never accept my money because she didn't agree with the way I made it. She was never a fan of dirty money, no matter how desperate."

Jax sat on this explanation for a minute before nodding his head. He knew how his mother was and Derrick was right. "So, what exactly are you offering?"

"The opportunity for you to make some real money and take care of the family. Nephew, you don't have to run around out there in them streets like a savage, or like the rest of them lil niggas, when you have the resources I do. "

His interest piqued, Jax said, "I'm listening," as he sat stonefaced.

"You see that beautiful lady at the desk when you came in?" Derrick asked, nodding toward the spot where she sat perched.

"Yeah, what about her?"

"Her name is Angela. Once we say our goodbyes, go over to her and very discreetly she's going to slide you a sealed envelope I've prepared for you. Don't open it until you clear the building," Derrick instructed.

"Okay, Unc, I got you."

As the two men stood, they grabbed each other in a loving embrace and hugged.

"Come back after you've taken care of all the business, we'll have a lot ot talk about," Derrick said cryptically.

When they parted ways, Jax left the visitation area and retrieved the envelope smoothly from Angela. He tucked it in the hip of his sweats and didn't pull it out until he reached the privacy of his Chevy. Opening the note, it read…

Dear Jax,

This is your test run. Follow the instructions written below and go collect '10 Bitches and The Black Book.'

4

STEP 1

FOLLOWING the precise instructions his uncle gave, Jax pulled up to his destination on "Dead Street" and parked in his usual spot at the end of the block.

It wasn't until Jax read the back of the note and arrived at his current location that he was able to put a few pieces of the puzzle together.

Now he realized, the man he visited earlier that day and knew as his uncle Derrick, was also the same man the streets called BIG D... The Legend!

Jax then came to the realization that the mission he was sent on wouldn't be a small one.

This shit crazy! he thought as he exited the vehicle.

The paper in his hand read,

"Step 1, #1 Go to my house located @ 112 Dead Street."

Done, Jax thought.

"#2 Enter the side gate to the backyard."

"Okay, okay, nothing too crazy so far," Jax spoke as he stepped into a yard of overgrown weeds taller than he was.

"#3 Take the bolt cutters out of the bag you were instructed to bring and cut the lock on the cellar doors, then enter."

"Aw man, here we go with that bullshit!" Jax fussed to no one.

"#4 Once in the cellar, take the sledge hammer out of the bag and crush the twenty bottom bricks in the far right corner."

"Aight now, Unc, fuck you got me into?" he thought aloud as he smashed through the old, solid bricks, soon uncovering a small black safe.

"#5 The combination is your C-Day. Once you open the safe, store the contents inside the bag."

Doing as instructed, Jax kneeled and blew years of trapped dust away from the dial. He cleared the dial by spinning it three times clockwise, then twisted in the appropriate combo. "Oh shit! That's what he meant when he said Ten Bitches…" Jax exclaimed as his eyes and hands ran across the neatly wrapped kilos of cocaine.

Being in the streets, Jax had come across his fair share of drugs, but this was by far the most white he'd ever seen. In person at least.

"#6 Now that you've secured the package, exit the cellar and go back to your car and prepare for step 2."

Jax left the backyard and went back to his whip, now even more determined to complete his mission.

As he rounded his U-turn in the cul-de-sac, his eyes observed Tha Spot and the abnormal stillness that surrounded it. It had been a week since the murders occurred at Tha Spot and things still weren't the same, nor would they ever be again. He knew that for sure.

Following further instructions in the note, Jax also knew he was on his way out of town. Shit was about to get good... Real good!

5

STEP 2

Jax floated down Highway 289 for about half an hour, going far west until he reached his exit some thirty miles outside the city limits. He cruised down the Levelland streets and shortly after entered a lavish gated community hosting tall trees, ultra green grass, extremely large homes and many uppity white people. Most of them carrying on in normal activity, walking ugly, but really expensive dogs.

As he rolled through the quiet neighborhood, he received numerous suspicious glances from the nosey homeowners as their eyes gazed curiously upon his old school Chevy, sittin' on twenty-sixes with the system blaring.

The uptight people secluded to that area were not at all used to seeing the urban vehicle within their precious gates. He couldn't help the unwanted attention. Despite all the extra eyes, Jax continued his path and eventually pulled up in front of a marvelous three-story home, boasting a well manicured lawn and a snow white Benz in the driveway.

Parking alongside the costly automobile, Jax began to read the note again to make sure he was on point.

"Step 2, Knock or ring the bell. Tina is expecting you. Nephew, get that 'Black Book' by any means!"

Hmph! Sounds a lot easier than Step 1 already, Jax thought, as he exited the car, making his way to the trunk.

Jax automatically assumed that when BIG D said, "By any means," in the letter that there could possibly be some form of trouble or minor complications, so he took precaution and retrieved his trusty 9mm for insurance. THE REAPER always came in handy.

His mind raced and wondered, as he approached the door. He wanted to know what a woman named Tina was doing with a book of such grave importance.

Jax's jaw damn near hit the ground when he rang the doorbell and a short, shapely woman answered, wearing sheer lingerie underneath a short and untied, silk Versace robe. She was stunning, resembling a sexier version of Keri Hilson!

She seemed visibly out of breath, as she placed a hand over her bosom to suppress the rise and fall of her chest. Jax noticed immediately how nice and firm her body was. Her skin glistened from fresh shower water, enhancing the glow of her caramel-colored skin. Her natural bedroom eyes were pure seduction. The woman in front of him looked delicious.

"Hello, you must be Jax. Please, come in," she said so sensually.

Jax strode through the double doors and was amazed by the high-class elegance of the home's decor. "This how the other half lives," he said lowly, in pure awe.

"Please, have a seat and make yourself comfortable, I'll be right back," Tina said as she waved Jax towards a couch in the living area. He was taken aback by the opulence of her place.

He sat back and sank deep into the wonderful softness of the huge sectional. His eyes swirled around the room, then found Tina as he watched her disappear up the twisting flight of immaculate wooden stairs.

He figured she'd gone upstairs to grab the "Black Book" so she could send him on his way. Little did Jax know, Tina had a special surprise for him. He wouldn't be leaving anytime soon.

Five or so minutes passed before Tina gracefully paced back down the stairs, as her sleek stilettos clicked in rhythm against the steps with each exaggerated stride.

"Would you care for a drink, honey?" she asked slyly, setting her plan in motion. She was a fierce lioness, hunting hopeless prey.

"Uh, sure. I'll take some water, if you don't mind," Jax decided.

As Tina turned and sashayed into the kitchen, Jax was overwhelmed by her effortless sex appeal and couldn't help but notice and admire the thickness fighting to escape the careless cover of her short silk robe. Each thunderous wobble of her ass cheeks raised the robe higher and higher.

Naturally, lustful thoughts automatically crept to the front of his brain, causing a massive erection to form, threatening to expose itself beneath the soft fabric of his Nike sweats.

Ooh, shit! Man, I gotta get the fuck up out of here… he thought.

Soon, Tina returned from the kitchen, holding two sparkling wine glasses full of deep burgundy liquid and sat them on the shiny marble table in front of them.

Seductively, she looked dead into Jax's brown eyes, laying her soft hand on his cheek and said, "Sorry, baby boy, all out of water." Then, she gifted him her most sensual wink.

Silent as a mute, Jax stared at Tina, his eyes wide then narrowing with wild curiosity as she took a seat next to him a lot closer than he expected.

The sweet scent of her Gucci Guilty perfume was absolutely intoxicating. That, coupled with her natural beauty and bodacious body, was driving Jax crazy. He was trying his best not to show it. All the sexual signals she was sending him sent him over the edge, forcing more blood to rush south of his abdomen, truly awakening his manhood. Jax was amazed at the effect this woman was having on him. She was easily ten to fifteen years his senior and strangely, she hadn't even touched him and he was bricked up!

"Uh-it's cool. I, uh-I," Jax tripped over his words. "I didn't really come to drink or intrude on your-your uh, date," he continued nervously. "I'm just here on behalf of BIG D to pick up the 'Black Book' and handle some business for him." He was doing his best to cut the sexual tension by avoiding eye contact.

Not willing to let this rare opportunity slip, Tina asked, "How bad do you want it?" while sensually rubbing her polished nails in an enchanting fashion between her luscious thighs. She could see clearly her allure working wonderfully.

Falling for the bait, Jax said, "Well... it's my direct order to retrieve this 'Black Book' by any means, so I would say really bad, I guess."

"Is that right?" Tina said as she took a smooth gulp of the fine wine and hypnotically rose to her feet.

Jax followed her every move as she slowly strutted over to an enormous TV screen and pressed play on a slender sound bar beneath it. Suddenly, the suave notes of old-school R & B slow jams gave more life to the room, enhancing the sexual ambience.

Completely lost for words, Jax sat there in awe as Tina began to shed her clothing revealing what the Lord gave her. What a beautiful sight to see.

Tina's body was truly stunning, all natural with no trace of surgical enhancements. Jax openly ogled her up and down drinking her in, as his eyes landed on the slightest imperfection on her almost perfect frame.

Just above the curve of her ass and the right side of her toned stomach, was a lingering scar stemming from an old severe burn injury. The detailed dragon tattoo crawling from her mid-thigh up her side blew a wash of intricate flames toward the torched skin making the accidental deformity look like a true piece of art that elevated her sexy. Still, Jax wondered how she'd gotten the burn...

In the zone, Tina moved towards Jax. her intentions now clear and to the point. Not sure what to do, Jax just sat still fighting to maintain his composure.

He was no virgin, and wasn't scared of the gorgeous woman stripping before him. He just felt a bit of guilt creeping into his mind assuming this beauty was his uncle Derrick's woman... Shiiiit, BIG D's woman at that!

Then it hit him... He thought about the emphasis BIG D placed on his "By any means!" statement, realizing what he must have been hinting at...

Finally, he began to relax and enjoy the spontaneous encounter as Tina straddled him and began kissing at his neck while simultaneously tugging at the drawstring of his sweats.

Hastily, she stripped him of his shirt, capturing the sight of his captivating muscular build. By now, Jax was fully aware of what was to come and was more than ready to go along with it. After all, it was his mission. A mission he would not fail!

Their hands and lips gradually explored each other's bodies, in no rush at all to finish the inevitable.

Jax's hands eased upward from his hold on Tina's slim waist and unfastened the lace bra concealing her gravity defying breasts.

He took one of her stiffening nipples into his mouth, vigorously rolling his tongue over it and appling great suction.

Tina threw her head back releasing a soft moan of pleasure as Jax sucked on her titties and caressed her ass firmly at the same time, making her love box drip with anticipation.

As the waterfall began to form between her legs, Tina knew she was ready for the kind of primal action she'd been deprived of for almost a decade!

She dismounted swiftly and fell down to her knees, reaching her small hands up his legs until she found exactly what she was looking for. Smiling with approval, she said,

"Damn, that's all you?" as she felt something long and hard as steel.

"Nah," Jax let out a small laugh, pulling out his silenced 9mm he'd tucked in his sweats shortly before entering the house. "It's all you now," he said, returning her smile. "Guess I don't need this kind of protection right now, huh?" he joked sarcastically, prompting a laugh from her then placed the weapon on the couch.

Tina enjoyed his sense of humor greatly but kept her game face on and progressed through the motions. She was on a mission just as Jax was. Her mission was quite simple, get an orgasm. While Jax was trying to secure the bag... by any means!

With THE REAPER no longer posing as a literal cock block, Tina's hands resumed their journey and graced the surprising length and girth of Jax's tool. She took her sweet time to admire his full erection.

Hungrily, she opened her juicy mouth and inch by inch took in Jax, making the majority of his hard dick disappear down her velvet laced throat.

Jax watched in awe as Tina's head bobbed slowly at first, then sped up as she began to suck harder and deeper, never losing eye contact with him. No doubt, she was a fuckin' beast!

His body had never been so relaxed or exposed to such pleasure. His eyes rolled to the back of his head and his toes curled unconsciously, as Tina licked and slurped all over his dick and balls until the sensation forced him to spill his sweet and sticky cum down her throat as she intended.

Even after swallowing every drop he had to offer, Tina

kept her vacuum-like suction on Jax's dick. She sucked him like it was the last time she'd ever be able to do so.

"Ooh, we're just getting started, baby," she informed after she popped Jax's polished dick from between her pouty lips. She then sat back Indian style and fingered Jax to come toward her with one hand as her other lightly danced down between her legs.

Completely turned on, Jax stood up, towering over Tina and grabbed both sides of her beautiful face, guiding himself back to her mouth and began to face fuck her with long, methodical strokes.

Tina happily continued to take all of him down her slippery, cum lined throat without so much as a gag, skillfully breathing through flared nostrils. She was loving every bit of this experience, honestly never wanting it to end. Truth be told, Jax felt the same.

Suddenly, Jax evacuated her mouth and pulled her to her feet, bending her over the arm of the sectional. Biting his lip, he then pulled down her soaked sheer panties, finally capturing a glimpse of her plump, hairless pussy, her sheen of juices all too enticing.

Tina's clit pulsated and dripped in anticipation of the much needed penetration. Jax teased her a bit, as he slowly rubbed her clit with the head of his dick for a few seconds, before he drew back and entered her walls with some resistance.

Only a few short strokes into her tight womb, Tina was already cumming. The grip of her walls on his inflated girth created a feeling of ecstasy for Jax he'd yet to experience with any female before including his baby momma, Cori.

Over the next thirty minutes, Jax pounded away on

Tina's pussy, bringing her to two powerful orgasms. Out of breath and feeling as if his lungs would collapse, Jax opted to trade positions with Tina and sat on the couch, enabling her to straddle him one again. This time she did so in reverse cowgirl.

Tina eased her way all the way down, allowing his sizable staff to overwhelm her body. In rhythm to the music that still filled the room, she swayed and rocked her hips, throwing her ass back into him with great strength.

Hypnotized by the view, Jax watched her ass jiggle up, down, up, down as she released foamy cream all over his extended pole. The thick film only enhanced her glide, probing Jax deeper with each bounce.

"Yesss! Oooh... Yes! Jax, fuck me! Fuck me, baby!" Tina cried out, now bucking back harder and faster as she felt her third orgasm approaching. She was in heaven.

Her sexy moans and motivational "Fuck me's" made Jax's dick throb uncontrollably inside her tunnel. He grabbed her hips and strongly tossed her up and down, punishing that pussy. For a brief second he could only imagine what good he must have done to be gifted with some pussy so phenomenal.

"Oh, shit! Ohhh myy, Goddd! Yess! Here I cumm!" Oh, baby don't stop!" Tina squealed and shook violently before she came and Jax simultaneously shot his load deep inside her spasming sex lips.

"Fuuuck!" He sighed and fell out the pussy.

Both in need of recuperation and maybe a cigarette, they just laid beside each other in silence for a few minutes before Tina spoke. "Not so sure what's inside that 'Black Book,' but I'm sure glad you needed it, baby boy. That was amazing!" Tina cooed and watched Jax dress while eyeing her total nakedness.

"Glad I could be of service to you. Now, I held up my end of the deal, can you hold yours?" Jax asked as he tucked THE REAPER back in his sweats.

Tina then reached under the couch where all the action had just taken place and produced a slim black book that resembled a simple men's journal. "Here you go," she purred and threw it at him.

Jax caught the book, smiled and nodded. "Well... I guess that's it, huh?" he said, not really knowing what else to say.

"I guess so," Tina replied reluctantly. She fiended for company and wished their tryst could continue through the night.

"It sure was a pleasure to meet you, Tina," Jax offered sincerely.

"Likewise, Mr. Jax," Tina said as she finally rose from the couch and slipped back into her robe, leading Jax to the door.

Walking behind her, Jax spared one last look at her bubble before passing through the double doors. As a parting gift, Tina gave him a soft peck on the cheek.

A cheesy smile was painted on Jax's face as he headed back to his car. Now that his mission was complete, he could see nothing but a field of dollar signs! For him, better days were sure to come.

But as luck would have it, those days would be numbered... Numbered for him and everyone he loved.

6

BLACK BOOK

TAKING A DEEP BREATH, Jax took a moment to fully examine the life changing article clenched in his hands. The compact black book was genuine leather, with a small numeric lock and revolving chrome dial on the side. It seemed extremely light in weight but apparently heavy with valuable info.

Jax fiddled with the numeric tumbler for a while, trying to crack the unknown combination. After numerous failed attempts, he realized he was over-thinking the code. Simplifying his thinking, he tried the previous combination that got the safe open... His C-day!

Nephew,

If you are reading this, well that means your time has come. By now, I'm either dead or heading into the very first decade of a life sentence. Either way, this book has made its way into your hands just as I planned. The contents attached within this book are extremely sensitive and are meant for your eyes only. So Neph, please C-careful with this. Protect this with your life because this is the ticket for you and the family to have a better one. Continue to follow my instructions down to the last detail. If I am somehow still alive once you've received this, come visit me as planned. If I am dead... Well, I'm sure you'll be smart enough to take the head start I'm giving you and elevate. You're a smart young man, full of potential. I expect great things from you! All the cards and keys you'll need are in a pocket at the back of this book. Now, you C-careful and make me proud!

Love,

Big D 11/30/03

Stash Houses. 1709 E. Hepburn, 1901 41st #C, 2626 26th, 611 Lasseter Ave, 5945 Stretch Dr. , 3430 81st # 120.

Utilize these stash houses as you see fit.

Accounts. Bank of America #222659904299951 PIN, 5563 Balance $272,354.27, #3117119950253246 PIN, 1870 Balance $103,497.38, West Texas National Bank #1995643201521932 PIN, 4469 Balance $49,853.65 Offshore Acct #2021429365 PIN, 2323X Balance $2,659,326.41 ...

Nephew, make wise decisions with this money. This is all that's left. Don't spend it all in one place.

Property. 4209 W. 50th, 2523 71st, 1717 47th, 112 Dead Street.

In due time, turn these properties into something useful. If anyone can, it's you!

. . .

Only two pages into his uncle's infamous Black Book and Jax already knew his life would never be the same. The third page of the book would only solidify that assumption.

Disregard the following if I am dead. Follow through if I am alive,

Clientele, 1. CHRISTO / Deliver 2 kilos this Saturday at "Level" 11 pm sharp.

2. Lil Vicc / Deliver 3 kilos every other Wednesday at "Wileys" 7:30 pm sharp.

3. Les / Deliver 5 kilos next Sunday at "Les' Pharmacy" 10 am sharp. *Leslie will pay half cash and half in pills intended for resale. Deliver the pills to GOAT at Tha Spot, he will be your distributor on that play.

GOAT is my main man. My most trustworthy set of eyes and ears in the streets. He will also be your muscle if any issues should arise. Call him when needed @ (806) 555-9196. If you can handle these few clients, I will see to it you get more along with more products.

Go prove yourself!

"Oh shit!" Jax cussed loudly as he read and re-read the mentions of GOAT. His stomach turned upside down, replaying GOAT's demise a week earlier at Tha Spot. Deep down he knew he fucked up, but there was nothing he could do about it now. He couldn't bring GOAT back.

Little did Jax know, Karma was preparing a special dish to serve him for the death warrants he issued that night at Tha Spot. In due time, he would know how it felt to be the one in front of the gun… but when?

7

LEVEL

Saturday was finally coming to an end, but the events of that entire day still burned fresh in Jax's mind. He'd found out his uncle was a notorious kingpin, had the best sex of his young life and become a multi-millionaire with a solid drug connection, all within a matter of hours. His life was taking the shape of an urban novel, all before his eyes. It was unreal!

All he had to do was follow the foolproof game plan BIG D was laying in front of him and he would surely become successful. Maybe not the way he'd always dreamed, but in ways he'd never imagined.

Around 10:50 pm, Jax turned down a bumpy brick road in the downtown Lubbock Depot District and parked his Chevy amongst a cluster of vehicles a block away from Club Level. Saturday and Sunday nights down in the Depot District were always turnt up. The vast selection of clubs, lounges and bars were always packed to capacity with drunken college students looking to have a good time.

Jax, being twenty-one himself, fit right in with the crowd. He was in his comfort zone, even though he had forty-thousand-dollars' worth of cocaine concealed in his Gucci bag, heading to meet someone, not even sure what they look like. So, for the fourth time that day he didn't know what to expect but simply went with the motion.

As he neared the club, Jax realized how long the line was and decided to try a stunt he'd always seen on movies and TV shows. Stepping up to the oversized bouncer guarding the entrance he said, "I'm here to see CHRISTO," in his most serious voice, with his chest puffed out and eyes full of confidence.

Country, the bouncer's voice boomed loud enough for the entire line to hear. "Well, my man, you gone have to wait in line and pay the entry fee like everybody else, bruh!" Then he turned away, giving Jax the view of his broad shoulders that read "Security" in glow-in-the-dark letters.

Jax knew how to play this game, it was simple… money talks! Pulling out two crispy hundreds from the knot in his pocket, he tapped the giant bouncer on his shoulder. "Uh-um," he cleared his throat. "I'm here to see CHRISTO," he announced again, waving the two big faces.

Now speaking the universal bouncer language, Jax was suddenly allowed access beyond the ropes into the club where business awaited.

Entering the double doors, Jax was immediately intro-duced to the loud music, searing body heat and stench of mixed alcohol. It was overwhelming, but usual.

Smoothly, Jax made his way to the bar and ordered a glass of Henny. His eyes rolled over the entire establishment, looking for signs of the man named CHRISTO. *Who the fuck is this nigga?* Jax wondered.

———

"Alright, alright, alright y'all show some muthafuckin' love one mo' time for the 3 Beautiful Girls! That was an amazing encore performance and believe me when I say, we can't wait to hear more from you ladies in the future. Now, y'all know the night is still young and far from over. 3BG done killed it and set the mood, so I gots to keep this shit goin'. Fellas, grab ya' ladies. Ladies, grab yo' nigga and let's turn the fuck up!" DJ Matrixxx's voice blew through the large stage speakers, catching Jax's attention.

At the mention of 3BG, his sister's group, Jax quickly scanned the place one more time until he spotted a familiar face. Standing a few feet away from the sectioned-off VIP booths was none other than his little sister Kam. She was cheesing ear-to-ear, entertaining the convo of some man who appeared twice her age.

Seeing that Kam was sporting a short skirt and a top that left little to the imagination, Jax moved at lightning speed toward her, quickly shifting into his overprotective mode. There was absolutely no way in hell he was about to let Kam make it. Fuck that!

As Jax crossed the club coming into her field of view, she looked as if she'd seen a ghost. Knowing she was busted, she immediately spit out the clear alcohol she was sure to consume, had Jax not crashed her party.

"Kam, what the fuck you doin' up in here and where's your goddamn clothes?" Jax yelled in fury.

"Uh, excuse you! Momma said I could come for the performance, remember?" she replied with sass while snaking her neck.

"Yeah, I'm sure she did, but not dressed like this! And she damn sure ain't say you could be drinkin' and gettin' all up in niggas' faces either! Fuck is you thinkin' … You only sixteen, you lil ass ain't grown!" Jax fumed while giving a cold stare to the man she was speaking with just seconds ago.

Trying to explain, Kam said, "But Jax, I was only trying to —" before he cut her off.

"You was only tryna make me kick yo' ass! Here go my car keys, it's parked down by the Hookah Lounge. Go wait there… Now!"

"Ughhh!" Kam huffed in frustration and stormed off, knowing there was no compromising with her big brother.

"Hey man, I don't appreciate you running off my guest!" the small, wiry, Mexican man draped in Versace said angrily to Jax.

Jax turned to acknowledge the thick accented voice behind him. Looking the man in the eye, he said, "Fuck you! Your company happened to be my underaged sister. I don't think you'd want to deal with the backlash from those kinda legal troubles, for one. And you damn sure don't want any trouble with me, for two!"

Normally, Jax would have tripped all the way out and fought the dude, or worse, but he realized he was surrounded by way too many eyewitnesses and had a rather serious felony charge hanging from his shoulders in the Gucci bag. To his surprise, the man replied, "My sincerest apologies, sir. I was honestly unaware of the young woman's age. Forgive me, but ya' know this is a club that caters to crowds twenty-one and up. My intentions were not meant to be foul or cause any harm to her. I was simply offering to help kick start her career, as well as 3BG's two other members."

"Yeah, at what cost?" Jax asked with high suspicion.

"A chance to manage the group, exclusively. CHRISTO has connections," the man stated boldly, patting his chest.

"Ooh, so you're CHRISTO, huh?"

"Yeah, that's what they call me... What could CHRISTO possibly do for you? Wait... Let me guess, you must sing too?" CHRISTO said mockingly, stirring laughter from his entourage.

"No, muthafucka, I don't sing. But since you think you're a comedian and you want to be a smart ass in front of your people, the price just went up. Yeeahh... I was gone bless ya' game for forty thousand, now I'm thinkin' fifty thousand fasho!" Jax said, ceasing the laughter from CHRISTO and his loyal counterparts.

CHRISTO's eyes gazed down toward the bag Jax held for a second and he quickly put two-and-two together, realizing his royal fuck up. Looking at a time piece on his wrist that easily exceeded six figures, he said, "So you BIG D's new runner, eh?" in an all-business tone.

"Jax is the name, homie! I damn sho' ain't here for no mutherfuckin' slave contract ass record deal."

"Well, Jax... I don't think my compadre, BIG D would like your attempt to shake down his most loyal customer now, would he?"

"Well, CHRISTO!" Jax spoke with exaggerated emphasis, "I don't think BIG D would appreciate your attempt to get his underage niece drunk either. So... Now you know exactly why I'm here, Fifty thousand or I walk. Then you're likely to have a problem you don't want on your hands, choice is yours, bruh."

After a brief moment of thought, CHRISTO said, "Close the curtains," to one of the burly men beside him with a wave of his hand.

As the maroon privacy curtains enclosed the group away from the view of the club's occupants, CHRISTO pulled out a metallic briefcase, suggesting that he and Jax get better acquainted.

Twenty minutes later, Jax returned to his car fifty thousand richer. He felt a rush he'd never before experienced. The aura within him emitting a power that was simply intoxicating. This one transaction only nicked the surface of his craving for more.

Kam waited quietly in the passenger seat, worried mostly about what her big brother might say or do. She knew Jax all too well and figured the best way to get her point across to him was by initiating the convo before he had a chance to. It was now or never. "Jax. Brother, I promise, I wasn't doing anything. I was just tryna help me and the girls get a —" Kam was trying to explain.

Jax cut her short. "Look, sis, I ain't mad at you. I know exactly what you were trying to do and I'm gonna help you do it. If you can just be patient with me, in a few more weeks, I got you. Trust me," Jax promised.

"But Jax, I —"

"Kam, I'm serious. Just chill and trust that I got you."

"Okay," she submitted, seeing the sincerity and determination sparkling in Jax's eyes.

"Now, one more thing. Kam, I love you to death. But if I ever... ever-ever, ever catch you out dressed like this again or drinking, I'ma personally fuck you up. Feel me?" Jax said with a thin smile as he mussed her hair like he did when they were young.

Continuing the drive home, maneuvering through the dark city streets, Jax knew he definitely had to make good on his word. The smile on Kam's face would be worth whatever struggle he'd encounter to do so.

8

WILEY'S

"GOOD EVENING, welcome to Wiley's BBQ! How may I take your order?" the friendly cashier asked as she popped her gum and patted the itchy spot in her weave.

"Yeah, uh-lemme get that number ten with them special house greens, potato salad and beans. "Oh... and hold the flies," Jax said playfully, laughing at the running joke the locals used there. Shit, everyone knew the flies in or around the building were terrible there, but the food was so damn good you just had to deal with it.

"That will be eleven-eighty-seven, sir," the lady said as she admired Jax's handsomeness, batting her newly purchased T-Mart eyelashes. Jax politely returned the smile and handed her a twenty-dollar bill, telling her to keep the change. His kindness further pushed her smile ear-to-ear, revealing her shining single gold tooth.

Sitting at the back of the restaurant, Jax devoured his fall-off-the-bone ribs and delicious sides while looking out the large window, in search of the next client.

As he finished the meal and rose from the sticky booth to throw away the trash remains, he caught a glimpse of a black-on-black Lexus making its way into the parking lot. Assuming this car to be driven by the man he was waiting on, Jax exited the restaurant and walked in the direction of the Lexus as it pulled up nose-to-nose with his smoke gray Caprice.

The Lexus was heavily tinted, but Jax was able to make out two body figures sitting comfortably in the front seat. The driver's door opened and a short, squatty guy with crinkled shoulder-length dreads nodded to Jax, confirming that he was indeed the man of the hour.

Hitting the unlock button on his keys, Jax nodded and signaled for Lil Vicc to get in. The parking lot was empty, save for their vehicles and held no cameras, but Jax felt the privacy of his tinted old-school was the best place for the conversion they were about to have.

*** "Wassup wit it, my nigga, they call me Lil Vicc. Ya' must be Jax?"

"Indeed. Nice to meet ya'," Jax replied as he flicked his lighter, sparking somethin' real potent.

"Shit, cuz, I talked to the homie BIG D 'bout a week ago. He say you gon' be tha one runnin' shit out here and all tha business he and I once had will now continue with you."

"Yeah, that's the plan. I'ma pick up where he left off, but avoid making the same mistakes, nah mean?"

"I feel you on that shit, cuz. Man, you know that was some fucked up shit that happened to D. That's exactly why I don't fuck wit these niggas and damn sho' don't trust these hoes... Lil Vicc ride solo. "

Exhaling thick smoke clouds and passing the blunt to Vicc, Jax couldn't help but ask, "I hear you on that solo shit, who that?" He nodded to the Lexus.

"Oh, that's just my lil nigga, Terry," Vicc offered as explanation and passed Jax the weed back.

Jax inhaled more smoke and gave Lil Vicc a look of unsatisfied suspicion. Picking up on the vibe, Lil Vicc elaborated.

"See, I know Terry and his folks from the Green Fair Projects. That lil nigga mom's named Sharon and see, she abandoned him and his older brother Terrance when they were real young. She pulled up over there and just left them with her mother Ms. Brenda, and nobody had seen her since. Well, Ms. Brenda had lung cancer and died 'bout a year ago and left Terrance as the only one to care for Terry. Then sometime last week, this stupid ass nigga Terrance gets himself murked, probably doin' some dumb ss shit like always. I swear, I couldn't ever get that boy to just chill and be still. You couldn't tell his young ass shit! So, now shit all fucked up for the youngin' and I'm really just tryna get that nigga to stay in school, eat, stay out of trouble, all that shit, you know? He young and I can tell he ain't built for this street shit like us. Shit, the nigga ain't barely said two words since the po-po found his ass the night his brother died. He been real fucked up 'bout tha shit. So, all in all, I keep him close to keep him safe, feel me?" Lil Vicc revealed.

Jax felt a weird vibe coming from the front seat of that Lexus. Like the passenger was glaring at him with ill intentions in his heart. But he quickly let the thoughts pass because of Lil Vicc's previous statement and because of the fact he was high as fuck and most likely trippin'.

"Yeah, I feel that though. That's what's up. Ain't too many niggas out here that would do the shit you doing," Jax admitted.

"I'm just doin' what BIG D did when he took me under his wing back in the gap. If it wasn't for him, I would have been outta there!"

"I see your point," Jax said, passing the blunt again.

"On a business note though, what's the ticket lookin like on them thangs, fam?" Lil Vicc asked.

"As of now, I got you for twenty apiece. All goes well, in due time I'll cut the price down if you agree to only cop from me and send any major lick you can't handle my way, after you verify that they are solid. That a deal?"

"Hell yeah, that's a deal! I'm 'bout to flood Parkway with this shit, my nigga! On tha' set!" Lil Vicc exclaimed, rubbing his hands like Birdman.

"Got the bread ready?"

"One sec. "

Lil Vicc got out and quickly made his way to his trunk to grab the money. Jax then got out as well and went to the trunk of his whip to produce the product. He initiated the process of opening the floor safe which contained the weight for this deal.

When Lil Vicc approached the rear of the vehicle, he laid eyes on the contraption moving mechanically in Jax's trunk. He was shocked, never seeing anything like it before.

"Damn, cuz! Wassup with that James Bond type shit you got goin' right there? Shit, you know a nigga out here movin' foul, that shit could do a nigga some justice," Lil Vicc said, leaning in for a closer look.

"Go holla at my nigga Hot Boi on MLK at Hub City Customs. Tell him I sent you. I ain't gone lie though, it gone cost a few racks, but it's well worth the investment. "

"Good lookin' out, my nigga!" Lil Vicc said, cradling the three bricks in his arms like a baby.

"No doubt," Jax said, "see ya in two weeks."

9

LES' PHARMACY

"GOD SENT YOU OUR WAY/To visit us today/So welcome you/New Hope welcomes you/Put your life in God's hands/He'll forgive and understand/So we welcome you/New Hope welcomes you!" The massive church choir sang beautifully as the organ, drums, and other instruments all come together in joyous harmony to carry out the tune.

"That is our special thank you for you special visitors that have chosen to be here with us on this holy day today in the house of God. I hope you are able to take something vital from the sermon I've prepared and that we may see you again in the many Sundays to come here at New Hope Baptist Church. We will always have our door open for new members to join our congregation. Now, today, the Lord above wants me to speak about greed —" was all Jax heard as he discreetly made his exit from the rear church door.

It was 9:45 am and he had a very important meeting with the last client on BIG D's list. A meeting worth a hundred grand. Jax told Mecia that his breakfast wasn't agreeing with him and he needed to go to the restroom in order to slip away. So, he had to make this last transaction quick and smooth.

Luckily for him, the pharmacy he was intended to meet Les at was only a block away, so he'd make it there by ten and finish up in time to catch the majority of the service upon his return to keep Mecia happy.

Shortly after leaving the church, Jax pulled up to the pharmacy and parked next to a solo truck in the lot. Although Jax wasn't a big fan of pick-ups, he couldn't help but admire this one. Its costly candy paint, gleaming rims and other modifications screamed BIG money!

Ding-Ding! An entry bell sounded off as Jax crossed the threshold of the pharmacy door. He took a few steps in looking around for the man of the hour and noticed a young girl around the same age as Ke. She was cleaning a glass countertop and other cabinets while bass boosted music blasted from her Beats by Dre headphones. Unaware of Jax's presence, she went on about her business through the store.

Suddenly, a deep voice boomed from the back of the pharmacy, "One second, Mr. Johnson, your prescriptions are almost ready."

A few minutes later, a strong lady built like a Hall of Fame middle line-backer, made her way to the front, eyeing Jax with some confusion. The lady was more handsome than cute, with a rich chocolate skin tone, deep dish waves and was dripping head to toe in Balenciaga designer clothing. In Jax's eyes, the woman was fly as fuck. He had to give her that. She looked nothing like a pharmacist. *But then again, what's a real pharmacist supposed to look like?* he thought quickly.

"Well, uh-you sho' ain't Mr. Johnson. You're way too young to be in need of this here Viagra prescription, so what kind of medication are you here for, sir?"

"Actually, I'm here with a personal prescription just for you, Les," Jax said, noticing her name on the pearl white name tag she usually never wore.

Looking down at the iced-out Presidential Rolex on her thick wrist and seeing it was 10:01 am, she now knew exactly who the young man before her was and whom he represented. All morning, Les had been so busy trying to finish the few medication prescriptions she had and rush back home to her needy wife, she'd forgotten all about the 10:00 am meeting with Jax. Most people wouldn't dare forget about a meeting so lucrative, but Les' pockets surely weren't hurting.

"You don't look like no dope boy," Les said to Jax, as she removed her Cartier frames and took in his choir boy attire. Jax stood there unmoved in his Perry Ellis dress clothes with his trusty Gucci bag draped over his shoulders.

"I suppose that's actually a good thing for business. I'd much rather these dealings between us go without much notice. I must say though, I didn't really peg you as a pharmacist either," Jax said in a smooth drawl.

"What can I say… Looks can definitely be deceiving," Les countered.

"True," Jax replied.

"Well, let's get to the business, shall we?"

"Of course. "

"I don't mean to rush, but I have a special someone I

need to hurry home to. You know how that goes," Les explained.

"Oh trust, I understand, I'm actually supposed to be in church right now as we speak," Jax said while rubbing imaginary wrinkles from his slacks.

"Tory… Tory!" Les yelled.

"Yes!" the little girl answered with an attitude that wouldn't be accepted in most households.

"You can stop cleaning now. I need you to go get that duffle bag from under my desk and then go start the truck."

"Why should I do all that?" Tory asked, surprising Jax with her blatant disrespect.

"Because I fuckin' said so! Now, don't make me tell your momma your bad ass ain't listening again. You know Sharon's ass is crazy," Les threatened in hopes Tory would cooperate.

"Ugh! I hate you," Tory screamed out, then stormed off mumbling teenage shit talk.

"You'll have to excuse my daughter Jax, she can be a lil uh-moody sometimes. You know how teenage girls are hell these days. "

"Yeah, I got two younger sisters, so I can understand what you be dealing with," Jax said, trying to build up a rapport with Les.

"So what you got for me?" Les asked, already knowing the answer.

"Five of BIG D's finest," Jax confirmed handing over the Gucci bag.

"Just like old times," Les said out loud, admiring the bag's contents. "How's D doing anyway? Been a while since we actually spoke officially."

"He's good. Good as can be considering his location anyway. Same ole' BIG D. only thing changed is the times."

Before Les could reply, a loud thud caught both her and Jax off guard, as the duffle Tory was sent to retrieve came crashing down at their feet.

"What is your problem, little girl? You are really showing your ass today, you know better!" Les flew off the hinges, raising her voice.

"You're my problem!" Tory yelled back as she exited the door with Les' keys jingling in her hand.

"Ooh, I swear that child is going to be the death of me," Les remarked, not knowing how true of a statement that was.

"This all me?" Jax asked, eyeing the duffle.

"Yes, but things are slightly different since me and BIG D last did business," Les confessed.

"How different?" Jax raised an eyebrow.

"Well the money is still the same five hundred thousand, all hundreds, as D was accustomed to. The difference now would be the pills. See, me and D did most of our business in the late nineties and early two thousands. A lot has changed since then. These days everybody is into Xanax, X, Percs, Mollys, Adderall, and Fentanyl... all that shit, so that's what I'm pushing now. Tryna stay hip to tha' game, nah mean?" Les reasoned.

"I see... shit, it's still gonna net the same street value as before, right?" Jax asked seriously.

"No."

"No?" He was confused.

"It should be more now. Maybe twenty-five to fifty thousand more, depending on how you see fit to sell it."

"I don't see no problem with that," Jax said as he picked up the duffle, doing the math in his head.

"Didn't think you would, youngsta. Now, if we are all good here, let me get to this girl out here before she decides to drive off in my damn truck," Les joked.

"Good idea, 'cause I gotta get back in this church before Ma has another heart attack," added Jax.

Heading out the door, Les said, "If you or your family ever need any medications, make sure you come get them filled here, free of charge of course. "

"Will do. Nice doing business with you, Les. See you again in two weeks?"

"Actually, if this product is as good as I think it is, I'll be ready next week some time."

"Aight then, that's even better!" Jax said as they went their separate ways.

As he made the short drive back to the church, all he could think while looking up at the giant cross was, *God is good*!

CHAPTER 10

THE FOLLOWING day after the profitable meeting with Les, Jax awoke from a deep sleep, feeling like a completely different person. His newfound wealth and power provided him with a sense of security and superiority he'd never experienced before.

Jax had successfully completed the daring task BIG D laid in front of him. Soon, he would be able to reap the wondrous benefits of his hard work.

Almost everything he needed to grow and build a solid empire was in place. He had he product, the know how and mental drive, but he in fact was missing two key elements.

One was the distribution factor for this drug enterprise. With thousands of pills and hundreds of kilos now available to him at the snap of his fingers, he had to find someone trustworthy to help move felonious products. On that ill-fated, murderous night at Tha Spot, Jax made the mistake of killing BIG D's right-hand man and main distributor, in an attempt to cover his tracks for the murders of several other victims. He deeply regretted his actions, now that he was armed with the information on who GOAT really was. Beforehand, he was truly oblivious to the role GOAT played in the streets.

Even though Jax's actions would hurt his uncle and temporarily put a dent in his dirty cash flow, Jax still felt deep in his soul he made the best street-wise decision, no witnesses! These days when murder was the case, no one could be fully trusted. His motto was, "If you can't count on 'im, draw down on 'im!"

True enough, Jax could continue to make the cocaine transactions himself, but it would take time for him to develop trusted clientele for the pills and it could become too risky. He understood that BIG D was putting him in position to become a boss, the king of kings, a true kingpin. If he wanted to ascend to the top of the game like his uncle, minus the federal troubles, he couldn't be on the front line of things. He had to stay behind the scenes pulling strings.

The second missing element was the muscle. With all the products coming in, money would follow in abundance. With vast amounts of both drugs and money, respect would be demanded. Naturally, on the flip side of things, envy was sure to be lurking around, waiting to rear its ugly head on a fresh target.

Jax was a man who could hold his own under fair circumstances, but he knew life itself was not fair, especially in the drug game. He needed help to balance all the bullshit. He needed numbers to really make his stake in the game. Loyalty had become foreign to most in this day and age. But, Jax happened to know two people he could count on, Greedy

B. and D. Lee, his best friends since middle school. They all grew up in the same neighborhood, within a couple blocks of each other. The trio had been through a lot since they met, everything from fist fights to shoot-outs. They got put down together and even went to jail for the first time together.

As kids, they always had a lot in common that kept them glued, but it was their undying love for football that brung them even closer in high school.

Back then, Jax, Greedy and D. Lee all played on the varsity football team since their sophomore year. Each of them brought a different dynamic to the team and possessed certain skills that made them stars in their 6-A division.

Greedy, who stood at six-three, two hundred-twenty pounds of solid muscle and raw power was known for his Marshawn Lynch style of running. At any moment, he could impose his will against any defense and dominate. Once he got his momentum going, he was not to be stopped by anyone until he crossed the pylons. Being watched for three years, he was amongst the top recruits in Texas for high school running backs. In three seasons, Greedy had broken the Texas high school rushing touchdown record and rushing yardage record, making him even more sought after.

D. Lee was a lockdown cornerback that could hit like a NFL linebacker. He was six foot one and weighed a hefty two hundred and five pounds. During his three varsity seasons, he broke the records for interceptions, interception returns, and forced fumbles by a defensive back. He even became the first DB at Monterey high school to win a team captain spot. A spot that usually went to the stand-out backer or defensive end.

Jax was the smallest of the bunch, standing only a mere five-nine and weighing one-hundred-eighty pounds. He made up for his lack of size with blazing speed, running a low end 4.3 forty-yard dash. He was extremely elusive and had the best hands on the entire team. He started at slot receiver, but filled in at running back and free safety when called upon. Jax was phenomenal at those three positions, but his famed speciality was kick return. Over his three varsity seasons, he racked up more touchdowns and yardage on returns than any other player in the country and completely shattered the school's reception records.

No doubt about it, they were all beasts! Everyone knew with their booksmarts and humble attitudes, they were college bound and farther beyond.

The trio managed to perform so well every year they attracted scouts from D-1 colleges, in and out of the state of Texas. After winning their second high school chips and their senior season concluded, each of them opted to accept full athletic scholarships to their hometown college, Texas Tech University.

They figured it would be best to remain close to home and family where they felt nothing but love and comfort.

Greedy had his mother and older brother there. D. Lee had his family and his then girlfriend was about to have his first child. A boy.

So, they made a pact to stay together and win as many NCAA championships as possible until draft day came and the NFL called their names. That was the plan.

Jax, Greedy, and D. Lee had everything. Love, family,

friends, and a full prosperous life ahead of them, until one ill-devised plan that senior summer changed everything...

One weekend they met up at Jax's house like usual and used Mecia's car to hit the streets and hang out. Everything between them seemed fine but things were surely different. D. Lee cut down the volume on the radio and broke the awkward silence first. He proceeded to admit he had not one, but two kids on the way by two different women. He was beyond stressed with no clue what to do.

Greedy chimed in and let it be known he was also stressed. His older brother had recently been arrested for an aggravated assault charge, which he claimed to be innocent of. His mother, Ms. Janet was shocked and had been crying non-stop for the last few days because she couldn't afford to get her son out of jail. Greedy hated to see his mother cry, but it wasn't much he could do to help the situation. Ten percent of a hundred-thousand-dollar bond wasn't easy to come by.

Everybody was going through some shit at the time and Jax wasn't excluded. His mother, Mecia had been diagnosed with an extremely rare heart condition and was in bad shape. Mecia was in desperate need of an operation she simply couldn't finance. To add to his problems, Cori was due to have their son Jr. soon and she was doing her best to drive Jax crazy. Since their break up, she'd been so bitter. In her mind if she couldn't have him, he'd be miserable. She started to create such a fuss about money, even when she didn't need it. Her family was well off and plus, Jax promised to always be there and provide for his son despite their split.

The guys were so down on themselves with all the

negative things taking place in their lives, they couldn't even see or enjoy the positives, like being the first males in their families to go to college.

After long talks and a few blunts of gas, Jax and his brothers came to the conclusion that the root of their problems stemmed from money. Shit was getting tough and none of their families were wealthy or came from money. Therefore, they knew no one to give them the money they so desperately needed.

As a collective, they figured the only way to help each other's unfortunate situation was to take some money...

That unwise decision is ultimately what derailed all their lives, changing the course of their ultra bright futures. The botched armed robbery failed miserably and yielded no financial gains. All the group received was a one-way ticket to the county jail and a cold cell with a looming prison sentence.

Their case and arrest was nationally televised and cast on growing social media networks because of the star power they wielded as top notch athletes. Once the college caught wind of the felony acts committed right in town by their future players, the D-1 scholarship offers suddenly disappeared.

Now, at that point, they were all left with no future and still broke, in the same boat, unable to help the family members they committed the crime for. Crazy how life works sometimes!

Through connections still unknown to Jax, he was able to get them all out of the sticky situation somehow, with the help of a great lawyer named Dillon DeCair who stepped in, in the nick of time and handled their cases pro-bono. All Mr. DeCair told Jax was, he was simply repaying a friend.

Greedy B. and D. Lee felt forever indebted to Jax. He was their best friend, their brother and would always have their back. Knowing all their history with one another, Jax made a call.

———

"Aye, what's crackin', cuzzo?" Jax greeted, as Greedy answered on the second ring.

"Shit, you know me. Just chillin' my nigga, what's the damn deal?" Greedy responded before he burst into a fit of coughs, then recovered. "What's good wit'cha?"

"Sounds like that shit you smokin' is what's good," Jax laughed.

"And you know this... man!" Greedy said, imitating Smokey from the movie *Friday*.

"Nigga, you stupid. I ain't fuckin' with you today, fam. Where my nigga D. Lee at?"

"Wassssuppp!" D. Lee said aloud before he started crackin' the fuck up over the speaker phone.

"Haha, I see both y'all niggas full of that shit today, huh?" Jax joked.

"Hell yeah," both men spoke in unison.

"Where you at, cuz?" D. Lee asked.

"'Bout to pull up on y'all. We gotta talk," Jax answered.

"Bout what? Wassup, fam, you straight?" D. Lee asked with a hint of concern in his tone.

"I'm coolin'. I don't want to say too much on this phone. I'll just say I need y'all help gettin' this money."

"Ahh, shit! Remember what happened last time," Greedy capped.

"Nah nah, this gone be way different. Trust me on this one."

"Alright, well shit… you know where we at, cuz, come through," D. Lee said, blowing smoke.

"Aight, one."

———

Shortly after the call ended, Jax walked through the threshold of Tuck's house into an opaque field of smoke.

"Damn, cuz, all you niggas do is smoke weed… pass that shit!" Jax said as he took a seat on the stained, sunken couch.

"What you expect? It's Monday … I ain't got no job … I ain't got shit to do!" Greedy high-sided and passed Jax the gas.

"Yeah, you got plenty to do," Jax stated then threw D. Lee and Tuck in the mix. "Y'all niggas too!"

"Like what?" they all replied with a curious look.

"Like I said on the phone, I need y'all to help me get this money." Jax took three deep pulls on the blunt and passed it to Tuck.

Before anyone could think of any smart ass replies or ask some dumb shit, Jax unzipped the duffle bag he'd received from Les and let them see the contents. They were all so high and in stuck in a cloud of THC fog, they didn't even notice the bag when Jax first entered.

"Ohh, shit! Nigga, who you done robbed?" Greedy asked seriously and stood up from the couch.

"Nobody," Jax said with a smirk.

Greedy gave a disbelieving look. He knew Jax.

"Nah, I'm forreal. I ain't took nobody down this time. This all me! Let's just say I'm well connected," Jax said.

"Well connected my ass. Hell nah, cuz, where this shit from? Better yet who?" D. Lee jumped in while Tuck sat quiet, lost for words.

"If I told y'all the truth, you still wouldn't believe it. "

"Try me," Greedy said, as he reached in the bag to examine the pills and bills.

Jax was quiet for a second. He was contemplating how much he could or should reveal to them. He figured he could trust Greedy and D. Lee with anything and Tuck was cool too, plus he had a certain skill set he would need down the line, so he had to trust him as well.

It wouldn't be hard to, the guys had known Tuck since middle school too, but weren't as close with him because he dropped out of school freshman year to pursue a career in the streets with his cousin, Tony Snow.

Tuck was the epitome of "dope boy," from the car, clothes and any other tell-tale signs. Jax knew Tuck knew how to cook up dope to maximize the profit on some of the bricks and he probably would know a few more niggas to purchase some work wholesale. So, it only made sense to bring Tuck within the fold too.

"BIG D," Jax finally said, feeling like he told the biggest secret ever.

"Man, BIG D been locked for a hundred years, nigga, everybody know that. So how's that possible?" Tuck asked, breaking his silence.

Jax then went on for about 20 minutes explaining how

his last week and a half went and how he came into possession of the narcotics.

Stunned by the revelation, D. Lee asked dumbly, "So
the whole time… this nigga's your uncle?"

"Yeah, I know the shit crazy. It fucked me up too, cuz.
We coulda' been on!"

"You always have been a lucky ass lil nigga," Greedy
said, causing a good laugh.

"So, what exactly do you want us to do fam?" Tuck
asked, rising off the couch.

With everyone watching him intently, Jax poured
forward into his semi-rehearsed spiel.

"Okay, so I was thinkin'. Greedy, since you the biggest
nigga in here, you should be our muscle or enforcer, or
whatever you wanna call it. Don't get me wrong, everybody down with us gotta be able to hold their own, but
when shit gets out of hand, I need to be sure your gun will
be the first to sound off. I'ma need you on pickups, deliveries and all that kinda shit."

"Say less," Greedy said with a smile. "That's right up
my alley anyway."

"D. Lee, I need you to help me by distributing these
pills in them strip clubs you love so much and some spots
down in the Depot. They already paid for, so we can be a lil
flexible with the numbers for now to build up some clientele. I'll need you for pickups and deliveries too. Always be
ready to bust your tool if necessary."

"Shit I'm wit it." D. Lee nodded.

"Tuck, I'ma need your help when the next load of
bricks comes in. I know you already be fuckin' around with
Tony, so I'm really just tryna help elevate your game from

crumbs to bricks. I need you to help me establish a wholesale clientele, as well as settling up some lucrative traps around the entire city, starting right here on the east side. We gone cook up a few of the bricks and flood the streets," Jax surmised.

"That's a bet, my nigga... Sounds like you got it all figured out," Tuck said before sparking another blunt.

"Almost. But there's always room for improvement. After I set y'all up to get rollin', I gotta come up with some kinda front to make all this shit look legit. We 'bout to be rollin' in the dough and you know the feds always watchin'. So, with that being said, until I get that part done and can legitimize our money, please nobody make any expensive purchases that scream dope!" Jax paused for emphasis. "Most importantly, if somehow any of us ever get caught up, stay solid! Forreal, be on some real 'Omerta' shit! I got a live ass lawyer who will get us out of whatever till we can figure out the next move. But, if we all move how we are supposed to, we shouldn't have that problem. Now as far as the money goes, everybody will be well compensated. A sixty-forty split for now. But when I repay BIG D for this blessing and we're legit, we'll go fifty-fifty... Deal?"

"We got ya, my nigga!" Greedy said, shaking hands with Jax.

"What 'bout you, Tuck?"

"I'm ready!"

"Shit, I been down since you hit the doe, cuz!"

"Alright then. D. Lee, I'ma leave this shit with you and let you get started." Jax slid the bag over to him.

"I got'cha."

"Tuck, be ready this weekend, 'cause I will be pullin' up."

"Say less," Tuck said, exhaling smoke.

"Greedy, watch these niggas and make sure they straight. Let's get this muthafuckin' money!"

"No doubt."

"Alright, bet. I'm out, y'all. Stay up!" Jax threw the words over his shoulder and made his exit.

As he backed out of Tuck's warped driveway, he knew things were about to change. That day was the beginning of a dynasty. Jax also knew things wouldn't be nearly as easy as he made it sound and there were more specifics to discuss, but if everyone applied themselves properly following the set stipulations, all would go well.

Now Jax had to go meet with BIG D again to set bigger plans in motions.

11

MORE THAN A FRONT

"So... how was the pussy, Nephew?" BIG D asked, smirking lightly. His VVS 1 diamonds twinkled through the part in his lips.

Jax was completely caught off guard by the straightforward question. He thought that part of the mission would go without discussion. Not knowing exactly what to say, Jax stuttered, "Unc, I-I-I thought..."

"You thought what, lil nigga?" BIG D slammed a thick palm on the table with a thunderous clap that turned a few heads. He fake grilled Jax, enjoying the look of confusion on his eldest nephew's face. A face of mixed emotions and a minute trace of fear.

Damn, I done fucked up bad this time, was all that ran through Jax's brain as he remained silent. Thirty long seconds passed under BIG D's stare before the man finally released the chuckle he'd been fighting to hold back, replacing the forced scowl.

"Hahaha!" BIG D erupted. "I'm just fuckin' with ya,

Neph. You did your job! And I 'preciate that. I'm glad you know how to follow simple orders. 'By any means,' right?" BIG D added, going back into his formal baritone.

"Right," Jax replied sharply, breathing a sigh of relief. He couldn't imagine fucking up an opportunity like this. Especially over some pussy. He just wasn't made like that! "Say, but what was that shit 'bout, Unc?" Jax had to know.

"Uh," BIG D gathered his thoughts. "Let's just say Tina has played her cards right with me for the last decade. And considering where I am, there are certain things I just can't give her. You both had something each other needed, so I set up a fair exchange. "

Jax nodded showing his understanding and approval of his uncle's tactics.

BIG D looked around cautiously to ensure they were still alone and out of earshot of others, sitting in the shaded outside visitation area before continuing their conversation. The area was occupied at first, but the occupants all scrambled upon BIG D's presence.

"So, how did everything go? D questioned before taking a sip of the soda Jax purchased out of the vending machine earlier.

"Everything actually was smoother than I expected it to be, but we did have two unexpected mishaps," Jax admitted.

"Okay, give me the details," BIG D said calmly. He was curious to know what exactly the second problem was because he was well aware of one already.

"Well... Unc, I hate to be the bearer of this bad news, but I guess it's better I tell you than hearing it from some stranger. Uh... GOAT... he's uh... dead," Jax paused for effect. "Someone murdered him at Tha Spot 'bout two weeks ago."

Immediately, BIG D's heart dropped into his stomach. This shocking information truly hurt. GOAT and BIG D had been thick as thieves for thirty years and hearing his homie was gone now fucked his head up.

"Two weeks ago, huh?" BIG D asked, fighting the pain building beneath his chest.

"Yeah... Somebody smoked cuz and a few more niggas. Cops say ain't no leads as to who or why yet though, I been keepin' my ear to the streets," Jax told him, totally omitting his true knowledge and involvement in the matter.

Soaking in his nephew's words, BIG D came to the realization it was exactly two weeks ago when he last heard from GOAT. He was on the phone with him discussing business as they usually did on Saturday nights when he heard a sharp whistle and the call suddenly disconnected. Assuming that GOAT dropped and broke his phone again, BIG D didn't think much more of it. Now he knew the sound he heard on the other end of that line was the sound of death, as bullets tore through GOAT's phone, then his body.

"What are your plans now for the distribution of Les' packages?" BIG D attempted to redirect the conversation. He was not about to get emotional at that moment in front of his nephew.

"I have enlisted the help of awesome guys I know I can trust. Guys I've known for quite some time, whose loyalty lies with me. Things are going to be a little different than you initially envisioned, but I will make it all work," Jax answered. He was relieved for the subject change. Guilt consumed him, but he couldn't let that show.

"I trust you and the decisions you've reached, Neph. Should things go awry, you have to accept responsibility for your actions and the actions of your clique. The game done changed. Niggas really out there snitchin like it's the thing to do. You have to be careful who you align yourself with. I mean, look where I am." BIG D motioned to his enclosed surroundings within the federal prison.

"Believe me, Unc, I understand the risk and reward here. Otherwise I wouldn't even get involved. I will be cautious and still ambitious," Jax said with a confident air.

"Tell me... what was that other mishap you mentioned?" BIG D asked, already knowing the answer though.

"Oh, yeah. Well honestly, that shit wasn't really a big deal. Especially in comparison to the death of GOAT, but I figured I shouldn't leave anything out with you. So you know I ain't on no bullshit. But oh, I had a lil issue with that nigga CHRISTO. I showed up at Club Level as you instructed, trying to figure out who the nigga was and I stumbled upon Kam dressed like she was 'bout to hit the stroll. Somehow, she ended up over at the ropes of his VIP section about to consume some alcohol he'd given her. You know like I know the intended actions of most men in the night life, so I quickly intervened."

"What happened next?" BIG D pushed.

"I made Kam leave and go wait for me in the car, while I continued to grill his ass. I guess he started to feel some type of way about the slight pressure I was applying, so he started throwing his name around saying, 'CHRISTO has connections.' So when I realized the name and that he was the exact person I was looking for, I decided to capitalize on his fuck up. I gave him an ultimatum. I told him the new price would be fifty thousand instead of the original forty thousand if he wanted to do business."

"And he went for that?"

"Yeah. He had no choice, I stood firm on that. The man disrespected my family and high sided on me, so it cost him. I had no way of speaking with you about the situation first, so I made the most rational decision I could think of, considering all factors," Jax expressed.

Smiling with pride and damn near blinding Jax, all BIG D could think was how much of himself he'd seen in his nephew at that age. He didn't take shit from nobody under any circumstances. Fuck that!

"He likes you," BIG D stated casually.

"Excuse me?" Jax was clearly confused.

"CHRISTO, he likes you and wants to continue doing business with you. Only now, you'll be the buyer."

"Unc, what the hell you talkin' 'bout?" Jax asked, on the verge of irritation.

Letting out a small laugh, BIG D spilled the Texas tea. "Neph, CHRISTO is the plug!"

"What!" Jax's eyes brightened with shock as BIG D continued to speak.

"I didn't tell you up front 'cause we both decided it would be best to see your true character on your first major transaction. The situation with your sister was purely a coincidence. What can I say, it's a small world... See, Neph, CHRISTO has many jobs, both legal and illegal. He is a talent scout for young models, actors and music artists, so that's why he approached Kam in regard to pushing 3BG's music. True, he was unaware of her relation to us and of her age, considering where she was at that time of night. But when you showed up and handled the situation the way you did, he really appreciated your mind frame and rational thinking. He admired how you protected Kam above all and didn't bow to him at the mention of my name. I guess he could sense you were solid just as I said you'd be. Unbeknownst to you, that night you managed to secure the connect of a lifetime," BIG D revealed in full.

"This shit crazy!" was all Jax managed to say. He was truly lost for words. Before the visit started, he was thinking he probably fucked up a relationship with one of his uncle's valued clients but that was not the case at all.

"Now that you've secured the connection with CHRISTO, I'll give you the remaining list of my clientele and he will give you however much coke you can move on consignment as long as you conduct good business. "

"Man, Unc, I really appreciate the both of y'all for granting me this opportunity. I won't let either of you down," Jax said with warm gratitude.

"All you gotta do is focus and stack your bread. You have all the resources you need to take care of the family and yourself. Make sure Jr.'s good, your mom gets any medical treatment she may need, and the kids go to whatever college they desire. I want you to make all your hopes and dreams come to fruition, Neph. "

"I got you, Unc. That's my word!" Jax said with emotion he'd never felt before.

"But there is one more thing I need you to do for me," said BIG D.

"Whatever, say the word," Jax proclaimed.

"I need you to secure an occupation... a job. I may sound like your mother with this, but I'm serious. You need a legal one. Or some business that will provide the income headed your way. You're going to have to gradually build and expose your wealth to look legitimate. You can't be broke today and rich tomorrow, Jax. I don't want you in 61 cell, next to me. If I were you, I wouldn't do anything too cliché for starters, like strip clubs or high-end car lots, or fancy restaurants. Do something that's not so obvious people will automatically know it's a front. Something they won't wonder where the initial startup money came from. Find something you love and will love to do every day, then give it your all. Hide in plain sight. Neph, you don't have to be rich and ball outta control, trust me. That's where I fucked up at. The reason I'm saying this and I even brung you into this is 'cause I don't want my family stressin' and strugglin' over finances. Y'all deserve to travel, go nice places and own nice things. Y'all deserve the world. Just please be careful how you do what you do and how fast you do it. Remember the IRS and the feds are always one slip-up away," BIG D let out in one big breath. He gave Jax some valuable game.

Before Jax could reply, BIG D asked, "Any idea of what you may want to do?"

"Actually yeah, I've been putting some great thought into that for a lil while and I know exactly what I'm gonna do. I'ma give Lubbock exactly what it needs," Jax boasted.

"And what's that?" BIG D was curious.

"I'll let you know next visit. Just trust, it will be more than a front," Jax smirked.

"Alright, well you C-careful out there. See ya' in a few weeks, huh."

"You got it, Unc. Stay up!" Jax stood to his feet.

"No doubt. Aye, before you burn off, grab that kite from Angela. It has my cell number and CHRISTO's. Make sure you call him and catch up, he's expecting you. Call me if you need anything else. "

"Okay, I got you. "

As they gave each other a G-hug goodbye, Jax turned back to ask, "Unk... how you get a cell phone up in here?" His curiosity had gotten the best of him.

"I'm in the feds, Neph, money talks! I can have whatever I want." He gave a wink and made his exit.

Leaving the facility, Jax thought about how legendary BIG D actually was and how grateful he was for this opportunity.

12

FOUNDATION FOR EVERYONE

THE STOMACH RUMBLING aroma of home cooked lasagna, buttered garlic bread and baked chicken Caesar salad filled the air, as Jax and his family gathered around the dinner table for another traditional Sunday feast.

Mecia led the blessing as usual and thanked the lord above vivaciously for her four beautiful children and the food she was able and fortunate enough to prepare. Sweet tea was sipped, layers upon layers of lasagna were cut, salads were dressed and breads buttered before anyone mumbled a word.

"Thank you, Momma, this is so good!" Jax said between quick swallows of heaven. Everyone's mouths were too full to sing their appreciation immediately.

"You're welcome, baby, I hope y'all enjoy it," Mecia said in the sweetest voice. "So, who's going first?"

Marcus took a big gulp of tea, wiped his mouth with the back of his hand and spoke, "Ma, I did real good in school this week, I got an A-plus on my reading test and a B on my math."

"That's good, son, keep those grades up and you will go far. I know how much you love your sports, but you'll always need a solid back-up plan, you hear?" Mecia smiled.

"Yes ma'am, I will," Marcus said, before forking more lasagna. He swallowed, seizing the opportunity. "Ma, since I got my grades up and haven't been in any trouble, can I please get the new Jordans that came out yesterday, please?"

"We'll see, baby, things are still kind of tight right now, but I'm sure I will figure something out in due time," Mecia replied, watching the hope in her baby's eyes dwindle. She hated not being able to give her children the world, but there was only so much she could do on limited funds.

"Speaking of back-up plans, I think I'd like to become a doctor or nurse if ball doesn't work out for me. I'd get to help people and make good money at the same time," Ke said as she dug into her salad.

"That sounds like quite the plan, darling. I'm sure one of those careers will work for you, you just have to put forth the effort and be dedicated to your craft," Mecia assured her youngest daughter.

"I was thinking that if I became a doctor, I could help take care of you," Ke said in a tender way that warmed Mecia's abnormal heart.

"Aw, you don't worry about me, baby, Momma will be just fine. Focus on your dreams and your future. That's all I need from each of you." Mecia eyed all her children.

At that moment, Jax felt it was the perfect time to bring

everyone up to speed on what his new hopes and dreams for the future were.

"I have an idea. A plan that if it works out right, will secure the foundation for everyone in this room to build their dreams on," Jax cut in with such glowing pride his chest swelled.

Everyone swallowed and dropped their forks in anticipation of his next statement. He had the family's undivided attention.

"As you all know, for the past few weeks I've been going to visit Uncle Derrick and we've had some pretty good conversations. He, along with the rest of you at this table, have motivated and inspired me to do better for myself," Jax spilled, looking at the faces watching him. "As a gift from Unc, I have received ownership of a commercial building property and ten thousand dollars to do with as I see fit. So, my plan for the building is to create the best recording studio and record label Lubbock will ever have. I'm going to call it Hub City Records. Now, the best part of it all is, the 3 Beautiful Girls will be the first official group signed to and managed by Hub City Records."

"Ahhh! Brother, are you serious?" Kam screamed with untamed excitement. She couldn't believe her ears. Jax's words felt like a dream come true.

"Of course, I'm serious. Don't get me wrong though, it's gonna take some hard work in order for things to flourish."

"Whatever it takes, I'm committed. Me and my girls!" Kam promised with tears of joy gathering in her sockets.

"All I need from you ladies is to stay focused on the music. Keep making great content and constantly build your physical and social media fanbase. Remember to be true to yourselves though and confident, always. If y'all can do that much, I'll personally handle the rest. I promise in time we will gradually rise and establish a spot in the music industry."

"Wow, son, I haven't heard you sound this passionate about anything since high school football. Are you sure this is what you want to do?" Mecia raised a brow.

"Yes Ma'am, I am positive. I know that if this works... No, when this works, we will be legendary and the material spoils and finances will be through the roof. I'll be able to put Ke and Marcus through any college. We can get you any medical care required and hopefully, I can get custody of Jr. or at least joint custody," Jax said.

"All of that would be so lovely, Son. I hope and pray this works for you. I'm proud of you, baby! As long as you're doing something productive and not foolin' around in those wicked streets, I'm behind you a hundred percent," Mecia voiced proudly.

"Thanks Ma, I'm so glad to have your blessing on this. It really means a lot because this isn't just for me, it's for all of us," Jax met everyone's eye, then continued, "Now, y'all know I love y'all equally, so I don't need anyone feelin' left out. Since Kam is getting the studio/record deal, it's only fair everyone else receives something too. Ma, I know it's been a minute since you've gone out and done anything women love to do, so I want you to take this thousand dollars and go get your hair and nails done. Maybe even a nice massage day at the spa or something. Just enjoy yourself because you deserve it." He reached in his pocket, withdrew a stack of bills and handed them to his mother,

her eyes watering. "Meanwhile, me, Ke and Marcus are going to the mall. Marcus wants Jordans and I'm sure Ke could use some new outfits for that recital," Jax concluded with a knowing wink.

More squalls of excitement echoed throughout the house from Ke and Marcus, as Jax soaked in the loving feeling he was bringing to his family. Mecia grew more and more teary eyed at her son's generosity. He'd always been a good son and she prayed that he stayed one. She had a gut feeling he was withholding something about the true nature of his finances, but she decided to give him the benefit of the doubt. He was her son, she had to.

———

Later that night, Jax dialed CHRISTO and they spoke for a spell before the drug lord suggested that Jax drive out to meet him. Things needed to be discussed in person. So, he headed to the man's compound.

When Jax arrived, he was greeted by CHRISTO's mafia-like security detail and searched. He was stripped of his weapon before they led him to an enormous, well-lit office, where CHRISTO sat in a large, high backed leather chair like he was the infamous *Scarface*.

"Jax, how are you my friend?" CHRISTO questioned in his thick accent.

"Thanks to you and BIG D, all is well. How are you?" Jax shot back.

"Look around... I'd say I'm doing pretty good myself," CHRISTO said rather cockily, blowing a train of Cuban cigar smoke.

"I see you. Shit, this how I'ma have it one day."

"Aw! That you will, I will see to it. As long as you are loyal to me and conduct good business, you'll never have any worries. That goes for the police and in the streets. That's my word!" CHRISTO pointed to the moist end of his cigar.

Jax nodded.

"Your uncle was a good man. Solid as they come. A man who stuck to the code no matter the circumstances. To show him my appreciation, I welcome you under my umbrella with open arms," CHRISTO said with such sincerity, Jax truly felt welcome.

"Thank you so much, sir. I'm really beyond grateful."

CHRISTO smiled, stubbed out his Cuban and said, "So, what kind of numbers are we talkin', Jax?"

Jax was quiet for a brief second.

"Well, just yesterday I received the full clientele list from BIG D and there were some big numbers on there. That, mixed with the clientele, I'm sure to gain on my own… I'm thinkin' at least fifty keys a week for starters."

"Wow!" CHRISTO looked over to Hector, his head of security. "This kid means business, don't he?"

"Good business," Jax interjected.

Everyone in the room shared a quaint laugh.

"Okay. I tell you what, Jax. I'll give you a hundred kilos on consignment today. You come and see me in two weeks with the cash. For you, the price will be ten thousand a kilo. This shit is so pure, if you wanted to step on it twice you could and it would still be the best on the streets," CHRISTO assured. "I'm not sure if you have a lot of stash houses already, but you're going to need a few more dealing with me," he said with a full laugh only the rich and wealthy possessed.

"Sounds like we have ourselves a square deal," Jax said as they both stood, made clear eye contact and shook hands firmly.

"Hector will show you out. Give him a delivery address and your package will be there within the hour," CHRISTO provided in a matter-of-fact tone.

"Will do," he spoke and continued his exit from the beautiful home.

———

"Wassup, fam?" Tuck answered on the first ring. Saying he was excited would be an understatement.

"Everything straight over that way, cuz?" Jax asked as he maneuvered through the inner-city traffic.

"It's all gravy on this end, my nigga. We done got off over half that pack you dropped. Shit, I'm just waitin' on you with that otha move."

"Say no mo'! I'm finna pull up and make it snow." Jax clicked the line off.

———

About twenty minutes later, Jax entered Tuck's house with an even larger duffle bag than the last one. D. Lee wasn't there like usual, he was out and about, trying to get off the last of the first pack. Tuck and Greedy were one with the couch going at it in a tense game of 2K.

"Threeee!" Tuck taunted as Steph Curry drained an impossible three-pointer from the half-court logo.

"Man, that yellow muthafucka always doin' that hoe ass shit!" Greedy grimaced in deep frustration.

Jax butted in quickly, "Man, fuck all that. Let's do this shit!"

Tuck dropped his controller and Greedy paused the one sided game.

"Let's see what we workin' with fam," Tuck was saying just as Jax tossed him the duffle bag, damn near knocking the air from his chest.

Jax and Greedy both laughed a bit as Tuck regained his composure and unzipped the stuffed bag.

"Damn! Nigga, you said make it snow, not blizzard! Fuck we gone do with all this dope?" Tuck asked, his eyes transfixed on the keys like a true dope boy.

"We gone sell it, nigga! Duh!" Jax stated the obvious. "I already got forty of these fifty right here sold wholesale later this week. So, right now the goal is to get these other ten gone. I was thinkin' we should break down five of them and set up a few neighborhood traps, you know? Put a few of the homies on, then figure the rest out from there."

"Yeah, we can do that. I just need to make a few cells," Tuck offered.

"Alright, just C-careful what you say on the phone. No slip ups!" Jax reminded.

Tuck grabbed the duffle and went to his cook spot in the kitchen.

"Aye Greedy, I'ma need you to roll with me tomorrow. I got something I need ya' help with," Jax told him, then snagged a blunt from the ashtray and put flame to it.

"Wassup, what you tryna do?"

"You'll see!" was all Jax gave in response, leaving his boy in suspense.

Jax sank into the couch and relaxed for a bit, enjoying the smoke. Two long weeks were ahead of him. He had to build the foundation for everyone.

13

HUB CITY RECORDS

"WHAT'S THIS PLACE, MY NIGGA?" Greedy beckoned wiping dust from the glass door, attempting to peek inside while Jax fumbled through the back pocket of the Black Book in search of the building key. They were at the commercial property BIG D gave Jax out on W. 50th Street.

"This place right here is our future," Jax announced, opening the door to the dark, forgotten building.

"What makes you say that?" Greedy wondered.

"I say that because you are now inside Studio 806, home of the newly found Hub City Records."

"Hub City Records?" Greedy was perplexed.

"That's right. This what I been working on. I told y'all we were gonna need a front, well this is it!" Jax beamed a smile of accomplishment.

"No offense, fam, but this looks just like some dusty ass building with some dusty ass rooms. Don't look quite like a record label to me. But that's just my opinion. "

"That's because you have to open your eyes to see my vision," Jax gamed.

"We gotta be lookin' in two different places," Greedy teased and broke out in laughter. He was still high as hell off a fresh wake and bake blunt he and Jax burned.

"Nah, but forreal, I know it doesn't look like much now, but with a lil money and TLC, we can make this the best studio in the city and one of the hottest labels in the game. It will take time, but I'm tellin' you now this shit gonna work. Mark my words," Jax declared. There was no doubt in his mind that things were about to pop.

"Shit, if you're this confident and you believe, you know I'm all the way with you. What all you need me to do 'round here?"

"Aside from our street affairs, I need one big favor... you still fuck with that nigga Stephen we went to school with?"

"Yeah, sometimes. He cool people. He be coppin' some smoke here and there and I be gettin' a few mixtapes from dude. Why, wassup?"

"I need bro number. You got me?" Jax asked.

Without further reply, Greedy pulled out his phone, scrolled down his list of contacts and sent Jax the digits. "Sent it," he said, "need anything else?"

" I 'preciate ya'. I'ma make this call, just hang tight and check the rest of this place out for me while I handle this."

Jax took a few steps off and dialed the number.

———

"'Ello," Stephen answered in a sleepy drawl, right before his voicemail picked up.

"Aye, wassup wit it, bro? This Stephen."

"Who this?" Stephen yawned and wiped the sleep from his heavy eyes. He didn't recognize the voice or number.

"This Jax, Greedy potna'."

"Oh, aight. Wassup, bro?" Stephen asked as he raised out of his bed, careful not to wake his sleeping wife and child.

"Sound sleep, I catch you at a bad time?" Jax replied.

"Nah, you good. I need to get up anyway. "

"I was callin' 'cause I think I got a gig you might be interested in... you still be fuckin' 'round with the music right?" Jax fished.

"Yeah I do, but not like I used to bro' bro'. That shit ain't payin' the bills, so it's not a priority like it was in high school. I got a boy to raise now too and I'm married, so I really been working non-stop," Stephen explained.

"I can dig that shit. Gotta take care of the fam by any means. I got a son too, so I know the feelin'."

"Fasho'. What kind of gig did you have in mind though? I could use some extra ends. Today my only off day from the warehouse, so I'm free for whatever."

"I tell you what. I'd rather show you than talk about it. Meet me at 4209 W. 50th in the next half hour so I can run it all by you. If all goes well, I promise you won't go home empty-handed."

"Bet that. I'm on the way."

With that they ended the call.

———

Twenty-five minutes passed before Stephen pulled up in the studio parking lot. The speakers from his family-friendly SUV knocked hard, carrying echoes of the latest trap-music. His wife's work badge ID swung from the rearview mirror to the beat, and his two-year-old's car seat clogged the back row, along with a sea of toys and scattered snack crumbs.

As Stephen exited the whip, Jax approached him exhaling bundles of smoke. They exchange G-hugs and a few words before entering the dusty building.

"So, what's the deal, bro?" Stephen asked, peering around the massive structure.

Jax let out a small THC induced laugh and gave Stephen the same answer he gave Greedy not long before. This time though, Stephen saw Jax's vision immediately and definitely wanted to be a part of it.

"You serious, bro? A real-deal record label?"

"Dead serious. And I want you to be our in-house producer and A&R. I need your help recruiting talent and handling all ends of the music. Nobody I know has an ear for music like you do," Jax admitted, hoping the compliment would reel him in more. Stephen was a beast and he knew it.

"I ain't gone lie, Jax, being a part of something special like this sounds very tempting. But I really can't spend all my time like that on a hobby anymore. I got my wife, kid and way too many bills," Stephen stressed.

"Trust, I understand where you're coming from. But I still haven't finished my offer to you," Jax added more bait. Stephen was Mexican on the outside, but he had more soul than most niggas. His well-versed knowledge of sophisticated studio equipment and ear for real music was impeccable. Under the correct guidance and backing, he had the potential to be the DJ Khaled or any other super producer for that matter.

"Money talks, bullshit walks. I'm so confident in your skill set that I'm willing to pay you fifteen thousand right now. If you —" Jax was going on before Stephen cut in.

"Fifteen thousand? Damn! You are serious."

"Dead ass!" Jax gave a straight face.

"Man, fifteen-K sounds good, that's a lot of money but it only lasts so long when you got—"

"The fifteen-K is just for starters. We will discuss future wages once you decide to sign on with me officially. On top of that, I'm willing to let you furnish the entire studio with the finest equipment of your choice. I want you to love your work and have the best quality of things to make your job smoother."

Stephen had to admit, this was a hard deal to turn down. He just stood there feeling like a kid on a snowy Christmas morning upon hearing Jax's full offer. In truth, he was in once he heard the word studio. The fifteen-K was a plus. But free reign over the music and production equipment was icing on the cake. He was barely holding his composure. "You got yourself a deal, Jax," he said, extending his hand.

Jax shook it. "I knew you'd be down. Things may start off slow but trust me, if you're here while we start from the bottom, you'll be rich for one and a part of history for two," Jax promised.

"In that case," Stephen said, pulling out a blunt from his jacket pocket, "here's to Starting From The Bottom," as he lit one end.

Feeling accomplished as pieces fell into their rightful places, Jax simply said, "Indeed."

PART II

NOW WE'RE HERE

14

6 YEARS

Over the next six years from 2013 - 2019, every aspect of Jax's life went from shit to sugar. Because of his pure relentlessness and determination for better, Jax and everyone associated with him managed to reach their full potential.

Just as Jax had predicted in the beginning, the newly minted Hub City Records label had blown up with blinding mainstream success. All while boasting 3BG as the cornerstone of the independent label. The growing artist roster Hub City Records maintained rivaled some of the top labels to date like Def Jam, Atlantic, Quality Control and many others.

Thanks to the undeniable success of the 3 Beautiful Girls' self-titled debut album going multi-platinum, in Texas alone, only a short year after Studio 806 was opened, a massive wave of traction was gained quickly for the label.

Also, 3BG kicked open the doors for a flood of other local artists in Lubbock like Bank$, Fudda Mayne, Love,

Tha' East Side Click and Jaquille to stake their claims in
the music industry.

Due to each artist's captivating and original style, work
ethic and fanbase, they all had individual success in their
respective genres. In turn, their accomplishments reflected
positively on Hub City Records and Lubbock as a whole.
Since Jax was the true creator of the entire movement, his
stardom grew rapidly.

Around their fiery fifth year of business, Hub City
Records began to land some big name artist from all over
the globe like, SZA, Yella Beezy, NBA Young Boy and
Mozzy. Along with OMBPeezy, H Boogie Wit Da Hoodie,
Lil Baby, Da Baby, Ella Mai, Roddy Ricch and more with
management contracts and record deals.

By year six in the game, it was clear to everyone in the
industry that Hub City Records was genuinely a top
contender with plenty of talent to carry the label. They
were a formidable force.

In that short timeframe, Jax had become a hometown
hero and a household name to the locals of Lubbock, TX.
Before his rise to fame, with his plethora of artists on the
label, Lubbock was mainly known for being the home of
the late Buddy Holly, and the college town of Texas Tech
University.

Jax's unwavering loyalty to the Hub City community,
generosity and positive outlook gained him love from all
angles. The amount of power he wielded in the streets and
the industry made him feared by some, but respected by all.
In his own right, Jax was like the second coming of his
fellow Texas native and hip-hop music mogul, J. Prince, the
founder of Rap-A-Lot Records.

All of Jax's family and friends reaped the benefits from the lavish lifestyle he created, especially Kam. She was now a beloved multi-platinum recording artist, Grammy award winner and actress, all credited to his initial push and dirty money. Recently, she even started a cosmetic line that was in fierce competition with the famous brands introduced to the world by Rhianna and Kylie Jenner. Kam was young, beautiful and by all means, living her best life!

Ke was thrilled by the direction of her life as well. She was now in her second year of college, attending Texas Tech University pursuing her masters degree in a medical related field. Ke was still an amazing dancer and often did back up dancing and choreography for 3BG's videos as well as other label artists. She easily could have made a fine living as a dance or choreographer, but medicine was her true passion now.

Marcus grew to stand six-foot-three, weighing nearly two-hundred-twenty-five pounds. He wasn't the typical high school jock though, he had both brains and brawn. He learned early on from Jax that he had to be strong mentally and physically to be a true success in the sports world. Now a senior, Marcus was the most sought after player in Texas and number two overall in the country. He'd received offers from all over the U.S., both academic and athletic. Marcus loved his big brother Jax and as tribute to Jax's shortcomings in college ball, he decided to forego his first option to play for the legendary Nick Saban at Alabama and he committed to Texas Tech. Although Tech's program wasn't accomplished as was Alabama's, Marcus felt his city deserved a fighting chance at a national title and he'd be the one to bring it on home, just like Jax would have.

Mecia was aging wonderfully and was in good health, for the most part. She was beyond proud of her children, especially Jax and the man he'd become. She truly appreciated his transition and the way he'd taken care of her and the family. Mecia spent most of her time now with her only grandchild Jr., and going to Marcus' varsity games across the state. She was still going to church and keeping their Sunday tradition alive.

Jax couldn't have been happier the way his life was going. All the cards had been re-shuffled and were definitely being dealt in his favor. He was legally a multi-millionaire, hometown hero and most of all, a great father and man.

After he'd begun to legitimize his assets and earnings in the streets, he took Cori to court again and was granted joint physical custody of Jr. Of course, Cori was pissed off because now she could no longer use Jr. as a bargaining chip to control Jax's life from afar. Jax's victory in the custody hearing didn't come easy though. Cori tried her best to convince the judge into increasing the amount of money Jax paid in monthly child support from the insane eight hundred a month, to an absurd five thousand a month, based on his astronomical income.

To Jax's surprise, the judge did not fall for the okey-doke. He stated to Cori, "Just because Mr. White can afford your requested expense, does not deem it necessary. The amount you've already been granted is enough for you to continue to fund you and your child's moderate lifestyle and care for him financially. If you still think you need more in support, let's grant full custody to the father and then you can send him eight hundred a month!"

That statement was enough to shut her up and finally accept defeat. For the moment at least, Cori always had conniving tricks up her sleeve. She saw Jax was happy, rich and single and just couldn't bear the thought of someone snatching up the man she fucked up and lost.

Greedy B., D. Lee, and Tuck were hood royalty. Everyone loved them, not only because of their products but because of the way they carried themselves. None of them got rich and turned their backs on the hood or started acting differently. They embraced the hood and everyone in it, showing mad love to its occupants. D. Lee and Tuck put niggas on to support their families. Greedy kept pussy niggas in check. Anybody who wasn't rollin' with Jax's growing empire had a choice, get down or lay down. The choice was a no-brainer for most, but of course some chose to learn the hard way.

To Jax, everything was perfect. But everyone knows life is full of surprises, soon he would find out just how many.

15

FALL FROM CLOUD 9

IT WAS A HAIR PAST NOON, as Jax layed comfortably in his California king size bed. He was in deep thought, reminiscing of all the good and the bad done in his life. Jax was at the point now where he had everything he could possibly ask for. Everything but a woman who truly loved him and deserved his love in return.

After his messy split with Cori, Jax never again looked for love. He had his flings like any other male, but his heart was never involved, not fully anyway… He just gave his all to his son, his label and to the streets. But he did have room to love someone special, if the right woman ever came into his life. Casual encounters just weren't cutting it. Some people would say he was trippin', enjoy the life of a bachelor. But he longed for more.

Between the smooth silk sheets and the thumb sized stick of "Gelato" he was smoking on, Jax felt like he was on Cloud 9. Releasing thick trains of smoke, he thought out loud, "Nothing can bring me down." Then his iPhone rang and fucked the whole vibe up. His fall began at that moment. Things would never be the same, the devil's advocate had already begun his work.

"Hello?" Jax answered with a throaty cough, the intense smoke violating his lungs.

"You have a collect call from... Tuck. . . to accept this call—" was all the computerized voice could say before Jax pressed five. He already knew the routine, having been in Tuck's exact position years ago. "This call is subject to monitoring and may be recorded. Thank you for using Global Tel-Link!"

"Aye wassup, nigga, what happened? You straight?" Jax rushed as soon as that dumb ass computer bitch quit talking.

"Man... I don't know, fam. I was at one of the spots for 'bout five minutes, handlin' some thangs right... Next thing I know, the door come flying off the hinges and 'bout six niggas rush in that hoe. I automatically thought it as a robbery, so I start—"

"Wait, wait! Don't say nothing else on this phone. Sit still and keep quiet. I'm 'bout to send the lawyer up there to get you," Jax cut him off.

"Cuz, that's what I'm trying to tell you... I was arraigned about an hour ago and the bitches denied my bail. I fucked up!" Tuck voiced with such worry. This was rare.

"Listen, whatever it is couldn't have been that bad. I'm sure DeCair can work his magic and have you out in no time," Jax said with confidence. He knew all too well what Dillon DeCair was capable of.

"You have thirty seconds left," the computerized voice reminded.

"That sounds good, but I don't know, bro. Just get that lawyer down here like ASAP! In the meantime, turn on the news," Tuck told Jax and hung his head low.

"I got you, fam. Stay solid!"

"On tha' set!"

"Thank you for using Global Tel-Link! Goodbye," the call ended.

―――――

Jax rustled through the covers searching hard for the discarded remote. With the press of the small power button, the TV illuminated the dimly lit room, casting a magnificent picture of the most beautiful woman Jax had ever seen.

For a millisecond he saw familiarity in her beauty, then he came to the real conclusion that there was no way he could know this model of a woman. But he should, shouldn't he?

She was very short and shapely, with sweet and innocent school girl looks, dressed in tight professional attire. Her long, flowing, light-brownish hair draped down over her slender shoulders, barely grazing her ample backside, her big inviting brown eyes looked like pods of amber on a warm day. Everything about this woman was a physical turn on for Jax. He was intrigued, captivated by her smile, a blazing broadcast of pearly whites.

Snapping out of his transfixion, Jax turned up the volume, only to hear his new crush deliver some harsh and unwanted news.

.   .   .

BREAKING NEWS

"This is Gabriella Renee, reporting with *KLBK Channel 13 News*. We're merely seconds on the scene here on the 2600 block of E. 1st Place, where authorities are saying that an early morning drug raid has led to a violent shoot-out with the LPD. This shoot-out resulted in the deaths of Officer Brian Todd and two unnamed suspects. The three remaining suspects involved, narrowly escaped death themselves following the hail of gunfire. Certain details and accounts of this event and the result are still unclear.

"What I can tell you now is the suspects have all been apprehended and taken into custody at the Lubbock County Jail. Each of them currently facing multiple felony charges for murder, gun possession, money laundering, illegal narcotics possession, and organized crime. Authorities are stating that an anonymous call coming in the wee hours of the night is what delivered the promising tip on this drug manufacturing operation. That's all I have for now, but we will give updates on this story as it continues to unfold. This is Gabrielle Renee, *KLBK Channel 13 News*. Back to you, Ben."

"Fuck!" Jax shouted in boiling anger. He threw the remote so hard at the TV, the screen shattered immediately upon impact.

"The fuck she mean, anonymous call? Shit don't make no sense!" he verbalized to no one but himself.

His mind raced in zig-zags one million miles a minute. Jax had the streets of Lubbock on lock for the last six years, running every angle of the drug trade. He started with CHRISTO's cocaine and Les' pills, but as his clientele grew, so did their taste in more potent and profitable drugs. As a result, he was now moving large amounts of meth and heroin. Those two drugs helped pull Jax's illegal net worth to a hundred million a lone. A major upside.

The downside of the deal was those same drugs carried a hefty amount of prison time whenever you got caught. Adding that, along with the arsenal of boasted military grade weapons and murder, shit was bound to go downhill.

Even though CHRISTO made a vow to Jax that he would never have any troubles legally or in the streets, Jax knew this situation was very different and maybe beyond CHRISTO's control. The drugs and the weapons were something that could be handled. A simple issue that could be washed away with the right connections and of course, the right price. But the murder of a decorated police officer changed the whole dynamic of the case.

Especially noting that this particular officer was a young white male, who left behind a young white wife and children. To make matters worse, every witness to the crime just so happened to be white police officers. This situation for Jax and everyone involved was beyond fucked up, but sadly, it was only the tip of the iceberg.

———

BIG D laid in his special double wide cell, furnished with a Tempurpedic bed, overstocked mini fridge, LED plasma TV and high speed wifi. He had all the jailhouse necessities and electronic devices you could possibly imagine, but none of those things could take the place of what he wanted most. Freedom!

He had a brewing plan to regain what he felt he should have never lost. It would take time, money and meticulous planning, but he would follow through or die trying.

His concentration broke when a soft, sweet voice attached to a lovely face and figure appeared at his cell door. It was a pleasant surprise.

Angela Rios was the product of an African-American father and a Columbian mother. She stood a touch over five-three, with long wavy dark hair, money green eyes and had a body worthy of a *Straight Stuntin' Magazine* cover.

She'd been working at the federal facility where BIG D was housed for the last nine years and since then, she'd almost immediately took a liking to BIG D. His story captured her attention and made her want to get to know him. The kindness of his heart and the confident manner in which he carried himself is what made her fall head over heels. So much to the point, she was willing to risk her job and life for him if ever necessary. Angela was truly his ride or die. Soon she'd prove it.

"Hey handsome, looks like you have a lot on your mind," Angela said to BIG D.

"You know me, baby, just brainstorming trying to figure out what else I can do to get out this bitch. I'm tired of this shit," BIG D vented, sitting up straight on his bed.

"I know, babe. So am I. But we just have to have a little more patience and this will all be behind us soon. We'll be having our honeymoon in no time."

"Did you get the doctor on board yet?" BIG D asked brightly, unable to mask the hope in his tone.

Angela deflated. "Not yet, I'm still working on it. I think I may have to persuade him a bit outside of these walls though, if you know what I mean. But trust me, baby, when I say, I will get the job done."

Weighing his options, BIG D just nodded. "I understand. Do whatever ya gotta do... Anyway, what you doing over here so early? I thought your lunch break was at 2:00," BIG asked as he got up and went closer to the cell door.

Angela looked around the empty dayroom and unoccupied pickett control booth before taking her keys and opening BIG D's cell. Luckily, all the other inmates were at rec, so they had a few minutes of much needed alone time. "Baby, I got some news for you that is both good and bad," she said as she entered the cell. "Once I learned all of this shit, I knew it couldn't wait so I took my break early."

"Okay," BIG D said, his curiosity piqued now. "Talk to me."

"How can I make this all make sense... Okay," Angela took a deep breath, "At about five o'clock this morning, there was a drug raid executed on the 2600 block of E. 1st Place in Lubbock. The team constructed and assigned to do the bust assumed it would be an easy one because there was only five occupants in the house and no one would be expecting the raid. Well, they couldn't have been more wrong. Two of the occupants inside the home immediately opened fire upon LPD's breach. One officer was killed from a gunshot wound to the head and both suspects were gunned down in return," Angel explained.

"Damn, that's fucked up. But I'm kind of confused. What that got to do with me?"

"Let me finish... I'm gettin' there," Angela said with a sassy eye roll. "So... The other four suspects in the house surprisingly weren't gunned down, but they were quickly taken into custody at the county jail. All of them were hit with a slew of charges ranging from drugs, the weapons and to top it off, the murder of a police officer. Now, the reason I'm telling you all of this in detail is because one of the suspect's names caught my attention when they aired an update on the news. Tuck Williams. When we first started our relationship you told me to be your eyes and ears on the streets. You told me to watch out for our nephew. Well, this guy Tuck, just so happens to be one of Jax's right-hand men in his operation. The same operation birthed by you."

BIG D sat there dumbfounded. The information Angela just dropped on him made his heart skip a beat. There he was stressing about his freedom, when in fact his nephew's and his nephew's friends' freedom were on the live. Before he could muster a reply, Angela said, "And that's not the worst part."

"Not the worst part, what in the fuck could be worse than that bullshit you just told me?" BIG D's frustration clearly building.

"Baby, don't shoot the messenger. You know I'm just trying to help. I refuse to leave you in the dark about anything."

"You right, beautiful," BIG said, leaning in to kiss her lips.

Angela continued. "So, knowing all that, I had to dig into the story further. You know? Just to be sure Jax was okay. The news reporter Gabrielle Renee stated that the raid was brought on by an anonymous call to the tip line. I know a few people in Lubbock law enforcement who owed me a few favors, so I cashed in on them to get a lead on that tip. Turns out the call came in about 12:03 am from an unknown number. I know this computer whiz guy from college who can work magic with this kind of stuff, so I had my source with the LPD give me a copy of the recorded call. Here, take a listen," Angela said, pulling out a slender metallic recorder compressed between her full, firm breasts.

She pressed play.

"Lubbock Crime Stoppers, you snitch on' em, we pick on 'em! How may I direct your call?" The voice of an over-worked dispatcher came over the phone.

"I need to speak with Detective Sullivan. I have a tip," the caller stated casually.

"Well, sir, Detective Sullivan is busy at the moment. I can collect your tip and pass the message along if you'd like. "

"No deal! I will speak with Sullivan and Sullivan only. Tell him I'm the C.I. from 'OPERATION BIG'."

"Please hold. "

"Sullivan speaking," the old grumpy detective's voice boomed.

"Sully, this is 'Blue Bird' from 'OPERATION BIG'. I have a tip that could do both of us some justice."

"Blue Bird, you must be in trouble again," Detective Sullivan half-joked.

"Not necessarily, this just needs to be done. It's for the best. "

"Well, what do ya' have for me?" Sully asked, his voice now dead serious.

"I want to report a drug operation. A real criminal enterprise!"

"What kind of drug operation are we talking here?" The detective's interest was high now.

"A major one! Ya know, cocaine, meth, heroin, guns, money and all that kind of good shit," the C.I. told all he knew.

You could hear Detective Sulivan's fingers flying across his keyboard in the background. "And where exactly is the location of this alleged operation?" he pressed.

"2600 Block of E. 1st Place, big blue house in the middle, can't miss it if you tried."

"Blue Bird, how are you aware of all this information?" the detective pried.

"Look, they usually do the pick ups around 5:00 am. If you strike then, you can catch them with the drugs and money together," the C.I. said, just before ending the call.

The information Angela had already given BIG D was enough to stress him the fuck out, for various reasons. But this shit he'd just heard on the recorder was on a whole 'nother level!

"Baby, do you recognize the caller's voice?" Angela asked.

"It does sound familiar. Real familiar, but I can't place a face on it. Who is it? I know I've heard that voice."

"I had my tech guy do his thing and he was able to reverse the *67 block the caller used to reveal the original phone number. Now babe, before I tell you exactly who the caller was, let me explain somethin' to you. When we began our relationship, I studied you and searched for everything I could pertaining to your case, so I could try to help your situation. Just as I do now. Anyway, I stumbled across some files the feds had on you. During their investigation into your affairs, they dubbed the entire investigation, OPERATION BIG. So, this same C.I. that is putting Jax in a dangerous light is the one who helped put you here as well... The number was (806) 555-0911, registered to one Victor Michaels."

BIG D sat there mouth agape in total shock, as the name rolled off Angela's tongue. A look of pure disgust covered his face. His nose itched from the stench of betrayal. Hate consumed his heart. He couldn't believe the man putting his nephew in jeopardy and help the feds build a case on him was his former protege, Lil Vicc.

"Honey, do you know this man?" Angela asked, peeking out of the cell to make sure they were still clear.

"Unfortunately I do." BIG D was clearly pissed.

"Well, he needs to be dealt with, like immediately. Do you want me to handle it?" Angela offered. She'd do whatever for the man who had her heart.

"Nah, don't you worry your pretty lil head. I got this. Thanks for puttin' me up on game, you've done more than enough," BIG D said as he pulled the woman close in embrace. "Now, I've got to call Jax, he will know how to handle this from here."

Jax just got off the phone with Attorney At Law, Dillon DeCair. Just as he thought, DeCair was able to maneuver Tuck and his workers out of the drug and other charges on account of a few discrepancies on the initial warrant. The murder charges however, that was something Johnny Cochran himself couldn't even get them off of.

It was quite obvious that Officer Brian Todd's murder was on the hands of the two dead black males at the scene. Unfortunately for Tuck and his people, being there when the murder occurred made them just as guilty as the trigger man, in the eyes of the law. Under no condition would the judge grant bail for any of the parties involved. Everyone arrested that day in connection to the bust and murder was about to do some serious time. Tuck's life, as he knew it, was officially over with.

Jax finally got out of his bed and got dressed. He was trying to figure out a way to make his next move his best move.

For the moment, his drug empire was safe from the looks of prying eyes due to DeCair's swift legal actions. That itself was great news. But losing Tuck and two other soldiers because of a snitch really fucked his head up. Plus, he lost a fresh shipment of drugs that was seized by authorities during the raid. And somehow, the two million dollars in cash that was in that stash house vanished into thin air, never being reported.

Jax started to think about who possibly could have called to tip off law enforcement, but no one came to mind. He had damn near the whole city on payroll and took care of those in need. He gave away money like it grew from the trees and used his ever growing platform in the music industry to boost local careers. Jax generously donated to charities, sent kids to prestigious colleges, and brought many famous stars to town for videos, concerts and wild parties.

It just wasn't adding up in his brain how he could be so good to everyone and still there was someone who turned on him. Six, almost seven years, had passed since Jax had to physically touch someone. The power he'd amassed pushed his hand for beyond those duties and he had plenty of people to take care of issues that arose like Greedy and his squad of young hittas.

Jax took this shit personal thought. When he found out who was behind all this bullshit, he planned to pick his guns back up and take care of that muthafucka personally.

His phone rang, snapping out of his terroristic thoughts. As he looked down, BIG D's name and face flashed across the screen. He took a deep breath, then answered.

———

"Nephew, we have a major problem," BIG stated as soon as Jax answered.

"Yeah, I know. Just spoke to DeCair, he's having the drugs, weapons and small charges thrown out, but ain't much he can do for the murder except shoot for a plea bargain."

"Damn, this shit is foul!" BIG D cursed. He took a dramatic pause before continuing, "But I'm afraid we have an even bigger problem."

"Another problem? Goddamn! What the fuck else can

go wrong? I done already lost too many potnas today, two million dollars and way too much product. This shit crazy!" Jax fumed.

"I know, Neph. This shit is getting out of control real fast. That's why the business I'm calling about has to be dealt with ASAP!" BIG D made it clear.

"What is it, Unc?"

"We have a rat. The person who called in that tip is connected to me and you. In fact, that grimy muthafucka is surely part of the reason I'm here and I never knew it until today. I fucked up and put him right in your circle and now your freedom maybe jeopardized for fuckin' with his bitch ass. He has to be removed!"

"What the fuck? Who is it, Unc?" Jax asked in both anger and shock.

"Lil Vicc!"

All Jax could do was shake his head, he should have known something was up with that hoe ass nigga Lil Vicc. About three months ago, Lil Vicc started coming up short. Twenty thousand here, forty thousand there. On the strength of Vicc's and BIG D's connection, Jax decided to overlook the money. He tried to look at it like a discount, so to speak. But when multiple rumors surfaced about Lil Vicc dabbling in a lil more than just weed and coke, Jax knew something was seriously fucked up. Lil Vicc was breaking the golden rule, getting high off his own supply. The nigga let some freak hoe named Roxy turn him out on that meth and he hadn't shook back since. So, Jax cut him off and banned anyone in the city from doing business with him until further notice. Now all the bullshit that was taking place was Lil Vicc's form of payback.

"I will handle it, Unc. I'll be by to see you soon to work things out."

"C-careful," BIG said, before ending the call. He knew Jax could handle Lil Vicc, but his gut was telling him there would still be more backlash and bullshit to come.

16

A MEETING WITH DEATH

JAX SPED DOWN MLK JR. Drive in his 2019 Lamborghini Aventador. It was one of the fastest in his fleet. He was on his way to meet D. Lee and Greedy in the hood so they could handle some business that just came up.

"You have an incoming call from, CHRISTO," the car's bluetooth enabled system chimed through the speakers.

"Aye, CHRISTO, I was gonna call you as soon as I got to my destination, but you beat me to the punch," Jax said as he answered.

"No worries, my friend, how are you? I heard the news," CHRISTO's voice held concern.

"I can't lie, shit is getting crazy and I may need your help," Jax admitted.

"I am well aware of what all has taken place in the last twelve hours. I've had my sources within the LPD ensure me that your name has not been brought up for any reason whatsoever."

"Thanks. Glad you still stand strong on that old vow."

"Always, my friend. I am forever a man of my word.
"

"I have another issue with that supposed anonymous tip, turns out it wasn't so anonymous after all. Seems for a while now, we've had a snake in the grass," Jax let it be known.

"Well in that case, I am prepared to have my people mow the lawn. No one fucks with my family and, Jax you are family. So point out the serpent!"

"No disrespect, CHRISTO, but this shit with this guy is personal. I have to do this myself. But I will need help getting a few answers out of him and quick disposal. Are the twins in town?"

"Ah, I see. Si, Juan and Jose are here somewhere on the compound. I can have them at your hand within the hour. Say the word," CHRISTO offered.

"Say no more, I'll hit you with the address shortly. Tell them to bring their toys," Jax said before hanging up.

————

Jax could almost taste his sweet serving of revenge as his moment for payback drew nearer with each tick of his flooded diamond Audemar Piguet.

CHRISTO's nephews Juan and Jose were complete savages and were sure to enjoy the grisly event ahead. They were identical twins, born to a Mexican father, and Japanese mother. Violence was a natural part of their being, it was deeply embedded in the strands of their DNA upon conception.

Juan was the brain, and Jose the brawn. Together they

would wreak havoc on anyone foolish enough to stand in the path of their desired goal.

Jose took after his mother. He was obsessed with their heritage and developed a love for sharp Japanese weaponry. Juan was a thinker, but also a pyromaniac like his father with double the rage and ambition. They were young and more than willing to prove their loyalties to their uncle's cartel.

———

Jax pulled up in the Dunbar area, in front of one of Greedy's spots' and got out. Greedy and D. Lee were posted in the yard smokin' some gas, conversing about some ordinary hood shit when they saw Jax approach.

The scowl covering their homie's face was one he hadn't worn in years. Both men knew shit was about to get real. They'd already heard what happened with Tuck because news, especially bad news, travels faster than the speed of light in the ghetto. But they had no idea how deep things really ran or who caused the shit, until Jax broke it down and laced them up.

"Man, Cuz! I'ma fuck this nigga Lil Vicc ass up! On the set!" D. Lee shouted while he reached for and then cocked back his favorite Glock 17. He was clearly upset that Lil Vicc pulled that stunt and tuck got caught in the crossfire behind it.

"That's some foul ass shit. You sure it was him?" Greedy asked incredulously, taking a deep pull of the Gorilla Glue.

"I'm positive. Shit, if Unc say it's him, then it's him. He

ain't gone play 'bout no shit like that. What really got my blood boiling though, is the fact this ain't the first time he done did some shit like this!" Jax revealed.

"What? What the fuck you mean?" D. Lee questioned with both anger and worry in his tone.

"Shit, you wouldn't believe me if I tried to explain how deep this goes. I'ma make his bitch ass tell you. We 'bout to meet the twins over at that nigga crib and handle up."

"You sure you want to be a part of that shit, my nigga? I can just pull up over there now and down his hoe ass by myself. Ain't no point of you risking getting in some shit too, we already lost Tuck. Remember, this what you pay me for, my nigga," Greedy said in effort to protect his friend.

"Nah, fuck that! I gots to be present on this one. This nigga done did too fuckin' much. Shit I can't overlook, feel me?" Jax reasoned.

"I feel ya'. Shit, how you wanna play it then?" Greedy asked.

"We'll talk on the way. D. Lee, let's take your whip, I'm in the two-seater."

———

The drive was only about ten minutes away. A straight shot back down MLK Jr. Drive, past Estacado High School, in a decent neighborhood by the Lubbock Airport.

It was broad daylight, but some extremely dark shit was about to take place.

D. Lee pulled his Mercedes Benz Limited Edition G-Wagon over to the curb two houses down from Lil Vicc's.

Jax had already sent CHRISTO the address while they were en route so the twins' arrival was soon to back door theirs.

A few minutes passed, then Jax and his right-hand men poured out the vehicle when an all-blacked out van pulled up on the block and parked on the opposite side of the street from them. Two identical looking men got out, made their way around to the back of the van to retrieve two intricately embroidered duffles, before approaching Jax.

Inside those bags lie the twins' work tools, small instruments of death. Neither of the twins spoke superb English, but they both understood just how to break the language barrier and get their point across. Death was universal. To Juan and Jose, causing a person to take their last breath as result of the tremendous pain they inflicted, was something to take pride in.

"Amigo. Uncle CHRISTO sent us. He says you require our services?" Juan said in a mixed accent. Jose simply nodded.

Yes, I appreciate y'all for coming. This won't be as simple as pulling a trigger. Believe me, I could have had that done without issue. But, this nigga needs to answer a few questions. I already know he's gonna try to play that stiff role with me, shut down and not say shit. That's where you two come in. I know you two can make men talk. I ain't got the patience to do the shit y'all do, I'll fuck around and smoke his ass. So, y'all ready?"

"Si," the twins said together.

On that note, Jax and the gang proceeded to Lil Vicc's front door, ready to set shit off.

Not long before his death, Lil Vicc was relaxing in the comforts of his home doing what he now did best, getting high! He was wide eyed, leading into his sixth day with no sleep, all courtesy of some high quality methamphetamine.

His life now consisted of nothing more than rolling bowls and blowing smoke. He was living carelessly off the eighty grand and two pounds of ice he'd finessed from Jax. Lil Vicc had no hustle, no family, friends or responsibilities. The envy he harbored in his heart toward Jax grew abnormally stronger everyday. The drugs running through his system only fueled the jealousy more. It'd been three months since he fucked up his connection with Jax and life for him had been downhill ever since.

The extremely potent drugs he now favored, often clouded his judgment, causing intense paranoia and his thought process to become completely irrational. Lately, Lil Vicc saw no wrong in his actions and doubly felt betrayed by Jax cutting him off. So, he turned to his old ways and began to slither. Lil Vicc felt if he could snitch and bring down Jax's organization, then he could assume control over the drug trade in the city, like he expected to when BIG D went away. He still resented D for never giving him the connect.

Sitting in his favorite spot on one of his sunken-in Lazy-Z-Boys in the living room, Lil Vicc's eyes were glued to his iPad Pro as he swiped at the screen. He was conducting his daily *Backpage* search for prostitutes willing to do whatever sexually explicit act he desired for the fair exchange of drugs or a few hundred dollars.

In the midst of reading a prime candidate's bio, he was surprisingly interrupted by his door bell. He had no idea who it could be, because no one in the city fucked with him any more. Reluctantly, he got up to answer the door and was stunned to see the man in front of him. It was Terry! The only person in the world he could even consider family. How could he forget that?

Terry had been locked up for the last year in Lubbock County, fighting some alleged assault charges. Before that, he was in and out of juvie as a teen and even spent four years in TYC. Now, he was nineteen years old, a grown man and free.

"Hey! Boy, I missed ya' young ass. Come here," was all Lil Vicc could think to say. He was too high. His week-long drug binge totally let it slip his mind that Terry was coming home. "Damn, son, what you doin' here?"

"What, you ain't happy to see me?" Terry asked, his eyes flashing hurt.

"Of course I am! Why would you say something like that?" Lil Vicc tried to sober up some. "I just thought you would have called so I could've picked you up."

"I tried calling but your phone kept going to voicemail, so I figured I'd just pop up and surprise you," Terry said, entering the house.

"My bad." Lil Vicc shook his head. "Guess I didn't hear it ringing. Sorry 'bout that," he apologized.

"Shit, it's all good, I'm here now," Terry smiled.

Together they embraced each other in a hug, showing a love that was father-son like.

"So, how you been, pops? The house looks good," Terry said.

"I been good, son. You know me, still gettin' to the money," Lil Vicc lied.

"As I knew you would be. Man, it feels so good to be free. I don't even know what to do with myself," Terry admitted as he flopped down in Lil Vicc's seat. He was still smiling, letting his newfound freedom sink in.

"Well, for starters, you can get your lil swole ass out of my seat and go check out that new stuff I got for you. It's back there in your old room. I picked it up a few weeks back at the mall in Dallas. I'm sure you'll like it. But shit, looks like you put on some real weight, so we might have to take a trip to exchange some sizes," Lil Vicc said with a laugh. He couldn't believe how big Terry had gotten since he last saw him.

"That's crazy!" Terry said.

"What's crazy?" Lil Vicc looked confused.

"After all these years, you still got my back, huh?"

"Always!" Lil Vicc stated seriously.

Truth was, Lil Vicc saw so much of himself in Terry, it was crazy. He would do anything for the kid. Terry was like the son he never had. Now that he was home, it made his fire burn hotter for Jax. He had to get Jax in a good way so he and Terry could live great!

———

Excited to see his new things and change out of his jail clothes, Terry made his way down the hall to his room. He was more than appreciative to have all the new clothes and other merchandise at his disposal. After looking everything over, Terry decided to lay down in his long abandoned king size bed and take a nap. He was a lil tired from the walk he took to get to Lil Vicc's from the jail.

Lil Vicc fell back into his spot, scrolling through *Backpage* again. Just as he found the one, the front door flew off the hinges.

————

"Alright y'all ... Stand back," Greedy said to the crowd as he gathered his uncanny strength and booted Lil Vicc's door in.

Swiftly, all parties crossed the threshold of Lil Vicc's home, resembling trained mercenaries.

Vicc looked like a deer caught in headlights as the face he hated most came into view along with others. Everyone he now saw in his living room had a vibe that screamed death.

The iPad Pro he was holding shattered when it slipped from his slick, sweaty hands onto the tile floor. A vivid display of a prostitute's ass and titties caught Jax's eye as he stepped within the semi circle formed around him and retrieved the discarded device.

"So…" Jax gave a long dramatic pause, "this is how you've been squandering all my cash, huh?"

"Jax, I-I…" Lil Vicc stuttered. His mind raced for an adequate lie.

"Shut yo' bitch ass up! You'll have a chance to speak in a minute," he said before giving a slight nod to the twins.

"Jax, wait, what the fu—" was all he got out before Greedy caught him with a vicious hook that put him on his back pockets, followed by a nasty kick to the head from D. Lee that put him to sleep.

When Lil Vicc regained consciousness, he couldn't tell

exactly how much time had elapsed. Everything was hazy and when he finally realized the position he was in, seeing every eye in the room focused on hm, he knew his time on God's earth was short.

He felt the bite of cold steel from the handcuffs restricting him to the table in front of him and the pressure of the chains wrapped around him binding him to a wooden chair. Underneath him was a large industrial grade plastic wrap that caused his stomach to turn. The whole set up looked like a scene from the show *Dexter*.

Jax stood at the edge of the plastic, side by side with Greedy and D. Lee, while Juan and Jose posted slightly behind Lil Vicc's chair.

The room was so quiet you could hear the pounding of Lil Vicc's heart. Breaking the silence, Jax spoke, "Now if I were you, I'd make this part as easy and as painless as possible. Just tell me exactly what I want to know. Anything other than what I want to hear comes out of your lyin' ass mouth, the men behind you are going to have a lil fun. Now you've been warned so the choice is all yours," Jax said so serious it was scary.

Lil Vicc let Jax's statement sink in for a second while he dug deep for strength. "Nigga, you a bitch! I'm not tellin you shit, so fuck you!" he yelled with courage and rage. He struggled with his restraints until he realized he'd never break free. Accepting defeat, he hocked up a loogie from deep in his chest and spit towards Jax's designer sneakers.

Everyone's eyes went wid in shock. All but Jax's.

"I'm not surprised," he said looking down at the glob of spit. "I kind of figured you would be stupid and say some shit like that to me. That's why my boy came prepared." He winked.

Lil Vicc continued to sit stone-faced like he wasn't worried about shit, when in fact he almost shit himself the very second Jax came through his door. Still, finding more insane courage, Lil Vicc sat quiet and mean mugged the intruders in his home.

"See, you could have made this a whole lot easier, but nah, your a typical dumb ass nigga. You let your larcenous ways take over and ruin you. You let greed and jealousy breed in your heart and create a demon seed. You bit the hand that was feeding you." Jax shook his head. "Lil Vicc, you stole from me on more than one occasion. I'm sure you thought I wouldn't notice, but I assure you I did. So, now with all that you took from me, it's time that I take from you."

On cue, Jose retrieved his favorite family heirloom from the depths of the fancy embroidered duffle and passed his twin a metallic canister and a lighter.

In one swift motion almost too fast for the human eye, Jose brung the short, sharp blade of his mini sword down on Lil Vicc's trembling hands with surprisingly great force. The quick hack sent threads of blood spewing onto the plastic as Lil Vicc's thick wrists were departed from the cuffs. Right behind his brother's quick movement, Juan's torch roared to life like a dragon awakened from a century's slumber and he began to sear the two rapidly leaking wounds to slow the blood loss and amplify the pain.

Everything happened so fuckin' fast and fluidly, Lil Vicc didn't even have time to scream before the deed was already done. When his ear rattling howl finally did escape the recesses of his chest, it seemed more so out of shock than pain. Terror flooded Lil Vicc's heart and he knew death was coming. The reaper drew closer with each passing second. At the moment he saw his mutilated hands, all he hoped was that Terry would stay put in the safety of his bedroom.

———

Terry tossed and turned in his bed as he tried to find sleep. It wasn't that the bed was uncomfortable, because it surely was. Especially compared to what he'd become accustomed to over the years. But his being uncomfortable was because of the recurring nightmares that plagued his mind as result of a few traumatic experiences he endured in TYC.

"No... Stop!" he screamed, clenching the bed sheets as he awoke, drenched in sweat. Gathering himself and getting up from the bed, Terry froze when he heard the most horrendous scream. To him it sounded like an injured wolf howling at a full moon.

Terry exited the room, wondering what the scream was about. Slowly, he crept down the hall and froze again when he came into contact with an unfamiliar stench of blood and burnt skin. He became nervous and goosebumps peppered his skin as he inched forward toward the source of the smell. Before he made it into the living room, he heard a voice that was all too familiar. It was a voice he hated and vowed a long time ago to silence forever.

Barely peeking past the cover of the eggshell-white walls, Terry crouched down and watched the gruesome scene play out before him.

"Hahaha," Jax laughed evilly as Lil Vicc shivered and tried to stifle his cries of pain. "Now that you see I'm serious and I got that off my chest, we can get to the real reasons I'm here... Tell me why you made that anonymous call about my operation to Detective Sullivan and tell me about your role in OPERATION BIG, nigga!" Jax demanded.

Just hearing those words, Lil Vicc could have rolled over and died. He thought his participation in OPERATION BIG was something he'd take to the grave. He knew if there was any chance of Jax sparing him before, it was definitely over now. So he played dumb.

"Nigga, I don't know what the fuck your talkin' 'bout!' Lil Vicc lied.

"Well then, let's see if my associates can't refresh your memory," Jax said and gave the twins a nod.

Before Lil Vicc could say another word, Jose turned in front of him grinning and slowly dragged the blade down the center of his chest, slicing through his AKOO shirt and layers of flesh. Lil Vicc screamed bloody murder as a cavity opened above his sternum and blood began to flow down into his lap like water down a riverbank.

Lil Vicc began to drift toward eternal darkness before the heat of Juan's torch burning his center mass brung him back to his harsh reality.

"We can keep doing this all night. I ain't got shit planned anyway. Or you can spare yourself further pain and embarrassment by keeping it one hundred for at least once in your life," Jax tried to coax.

Lil Vicc was already missing both hands, had a nasty

gash in his chest, his jaw was swollen and his right eye shut. In his mind, he was so fucked up there was no point in giving in now. He felt like, *fuck it, I'm gonna die anyway.* So he said, "Fuck ya, Jax!" and spit at him again.

Before anyone could stop him, Jax flew across the plastic covered floor and proceeded to beat the shit out of Lil Vicc. He threw punch after punch, yelling, "If you would have been this stiff with the laws, I wouldn't be here bitch ass, snitch ass nigga!"

Soon enough, D. Lee managed to get Jax off Lil Vicc and calm down. He whispered, "If we stick to the script and let the twins work, eventually Lil Vicc would crack."

Lil Vicc was determined not to fold. He figured it was a small form of payback by holding out on Jax and not giving him the answers he sought. Through his beaten and bloody eyes, he saw a flash of movement in the distance of the hall the made him change his entire demeanor.

A teary-eyed Terry, was crouched behind the wall, witnessing everything. That instant, Lil Vicc knew he had to come clean and keep all the attention on him by giving Jax what he came for. If for some reason they got fed up with him and decided to look around for answers, they wouldn't find any but they could find Terry and that would hurt his soul to see harm done to the kid.

"Fuck it! Strip him," Jax ordered.

"Alright," Lil Vicc spit blood and coughed, "Just chill… I'll tell you everything."

Jax raised a hand to stop Juan and Jose.

"You damn sure better or you ain't gone like what happens next!"

Lil Vicc breathed heavily. "OPERATION BIG wasn't my fault."

"Fuck you mean, it wasn't your fault, nigga? Who's fuckin' fault was it?"

Hesitantly, Lil Vicc said, "It was all on GOAT. "

"Hell, nah! Nigga, you lyin'!" Jax didn't believe that shit for one second. GOAT would never do some hoe shit like rat.

"I'm serious," Lil Vicc pleaded. "Look, Jax, this is how it all happened," he said and stole a quick unnoticed look at Terry. "Back in the gap, me and GOAT was down with your uncle touch. Just like you and them," he nodded to Greedy and D. Lee. "Me and GOAT used to do all the pick-ups. Same amounts, same day of the month. We had a schedule and route we stuck to. Everything was easy and smooth. Then one day, everything changed and BIG D had us moving different. All seemed good at first, but one time after getting the load, shit went bad. Me and GOAT were en route to the safe house when we get stopped. We played it cool of course, but GOAT was high as fuck and the law said he'd stopped us because GOAT was swervin' and shit. The officer's name was Sullivan."

Jax recognized the name immediately as Lil Vicc recounted the story.

"You know how the laws in the 806 are, man. He asked us to step out the car, handled us all rough and searched the car, even though we never gave permission. Somehow, the officer found the secret compartment with all the dope and that's when shit got real. We get arrested and he takes us down to the station downtown. The whole ride there I was nervous but I stayed quiet cause I didn't know what the hell to say. Truth is, I was scared then a bitch! But GOAT, he was pissed! That nigga was trippin', sayin' shit like, "Man, I gotta baby on the way, I ain't goin' down for this shit. So, anyway we get to the station, get booked and put in this room together. After a while, Sullivan comes into the interrogation room with this fine ass lady named Vivian Anderson who turned out to be DEA. They grilled the shit out of GOAT for info on who our boss was and in no time, he rolled on BIG D right in front of me, telling all he knew. Then the nigga offered to set BIG D up with Vivian in exchange for our freedom," Lil Vicc admitted with his head down.

"Nah, nigga, don't try to blame all this on a dead man. I know you played more of a part in it, that shit ain't happen like that," Jax argued.

"Jax, look, you have to understand the only reason I went along with everything GOAT was saying is because before the laws came in, GOAT said he'd kill me if I didn't. And I know he would have too! That nigga was crazy! I can only imagine what he may have done to me back then. This ain't shit!" he said, raising the nubs of his wrists. "He said it was only fair BIG D take the fall because we were the ones putting in all the work, yet he was the only millionaire of the bunch. Man I was only seventeen years —"

Jax had heard enough. "I don't give a fuck if you were seventeen or seventy, nigga! You knew the rules when you got in the game. Y'all got caught! So, y'all were supposed to fade whatever came with that shit. Instead, both you bitch ass niggas caught that pussy and traded my uncle's life for yours… Sad thing is I used to feel bad about the night I killed GOAT at Tha Spot. Now, I wish I could do it again with a clear conscience," Jax expressed. "Greedy, let me see the strap," Jax said through clenched teeth.

Greedy produced a sleek Smith and Wesson .40 and handed it to his potna.

Jax cocked it, pointed it at Lil Vicc and delivered a final message, "When you get to wherever it is we go when we die, tell that bitch ass nigga GOAT I send my regards!" Then he pulled the trigger, putting a hole in the middle of Lil Vicc's forehead. The slump of his body brought Jax relief.

Their ritual after any death they caused or took part in, Juan and Jose moved to dismember Lil Vicc's body and wrap it in the pre-laid plastic for easier removal. Only God knows where they'd take the corpse and what'd become of it. The twins were somewhat disappointed they didn't get to go as hard as they normally did on other victims, but they understood this wasn't about them, this kill was personal to Jax.

"Now what, my nigga? Greedy asked while he, D. Lee and Jax watched the twins work.

"Now, everything is back to normal. We are going to have to be more careful and cautious because of what happened with my boy Tuck though," Jax shook his head. "We should be straight now that we have gotten rid of the rat infestation. Let's get the fuck up outta here, we gotta be back at the studio early tomorrow, 3BG should be back from tour and we have a lot on the new schedule."

17

THE INFILTRATION

DURING HIS INCARCERATION, Terry daydreamed constantly of the day he'd finally get to even the score with Jax. But he never once thought he would have to suffer yet another devastating blow before the opportunity arose.

Over the years, Terry studied everything he could in relation to Jax. He watched his TV interviews, his rags-to-riches life documentary, read magazine features and just about every article published about him in the *Lubbock Avalanche Journal*. He came to know Jax like the back of his hand and understood that the key to ultimate revenge with Jax was to break the man down by attacking what he adored most, his friends and family!

————

When Jax and his cohorts left Lil Vicc's house, Terry exited the cover of his hiding place cautiously as though the men might double back. He was beyond hurt. There wasn't an exact word to describe the rage building within him. Once again, Jax had managed to viciously murder the only person he could call family, leaving him lost and alone.

Terry walked over to the now empty spot on the floor where Lil Vicc was executed. He dropped to his knees and began to weep, weakly. The first tears he'd shed in years. After letting all of his sorrows pass, he gathered himself and checked his emotions.

Ready to do something about the situation at hand, he began to go through the house in search of anything helpful he could use in his light for revenge.

Lil Vicc was never good at hiding things and in no time, Terry had uncovered a small pistol, a few stacks of cash and a mini duffle filled to the brim with crystal shards in clear plastic bags. Being lame to the drug game, he had no idea what to do with the drugs but he would soon figure it out. See, Terry had one thing going for him at least. He knew exactly where Jax was scheduled to be the following day, so he had enough time to strategize his infiltration.

––––––––

"Hey Larry, what's up?" Roxy asked, as she exited the Game Room door and saw her on-again, off-again smoke buddy.

"Girrrl," he drawled out, "what the fuck you want?" annoyance in his tone clear as day. He reluctantly showed his face to hear her out, though he already knew what she wanted. It was always the same with Roxy.

"Uhn-uhn, I know that walk, bitch. Don't be tryna play me... I know you holdin' somethin'. Ain't you gonna smoke with me?" Roxy said with big pleading eyes. She'd just lost her last twenty dollars on the Life of Luxury slots inside the semi-legal gambling establishment in a fool's attempt to gain more funds to feed her growing habit.

For less than a second, Larry looked like he was giving her question some thought before he selfishly denied her request. "Ain't nobody got time to be dealin' with your freaky ass today, Roxy," he stated in an overly girlish voice. "But I tell you what, there's this new dealer over there down by the studio and girrrl, he's practically giving dope away like it's candy! You better go get it while the gettin's good. He gave me all this for fifty dollars," Larry said proudly, showing Roxy a handful of shards easily, worth five hundred dollars.

"Damn! All that for fifty dollars? The shit must be bunk or somethin," Roxy remarked, eyeing the dope suspiciously.

"Well, I'm damn sure about to go and find out. If I were you, I'd go talk to him and find out too," Larry said and turned to walk off.

Roxy grabbed a shoulder and stopped him. "But I ain't got no more money," she confided sadly.

"Bitch, since when have you ever needed any!" Larry let his eyes linger over her lower half, before giving her a wink. Then he turned and walked off again, switching way harder than men should be capable of.

———

Terry stood up against the rugged brick wall behind him with one leg kicked back to prop him up. In his mind, he was playing the role of a dope boy. He was within spitting distance of Studio 806's doors and was quite nervous with the plan he'd set in motion.

Smoke from the Newport 100 he'd lit waved around his frame as he inhaled and exhaled in rhythm. Since his arrival to the studio premises an hour or so prior, fiends had been flocking to him like flies to shit. He blessed one lucky fiend with a gram and told him to spread the word and once the smokers were hip to the best dope in the city, the action was non-stop. He could have easily hung out in that same spot all day and made some real money hand over fist if he knew the game. But the money wasn't his goal anyway. His plan ran much deeper, but his patience was wearing thin.

As his cigarette reached the filter, Terry took one last drag and flicked the butt into the small pile he'd already created. Taking in his surroundings, he came to lock eyes with a very shapely woman headed in his direction.

Before the methamphetamine epidemic plagued the city of Lubbock and many other states and cities alike, Roxy was what most men would call a dime piece or labeled a "bad bitch." She was Puerto Rican. Stood five-two, with a flat stomach, thick thighs, beautiful light-gray eyes, double-Ds, perfect teeth and flaunted an ass that made both men and women stare.

Nowadays, as a result of hard living and overindulging in hard drugs, Roxy's beauty started to deteriorate. Her once plump cheeks began to sink in, her eye-catching breasts started to sag and her teeth had definitely seen better days. Luckily though, by some unknown miracle, her bodacious ass never changed and became her biggest asset. In the drug scene, that ass often gave her the boost she needed to acquire what she desired. Any chance she got to use it to her advantage, she did so without shame.

"Hello, Mr. Man." She stepped to Terry. "A lil birdie told me you got just what I'm lookin' for." Roxy batted her lashes. She admired his boyish good looks. Right away she could tell he was young, but he was playing a grown man's game, so he wouldn't be off limits to her seduction attempts.

"Yeah, I got you for fifty or better," Terry said while trying to avoid eye contact, sounding like a seasoned corner boy.

Roxy dug into the depths of her bosom in effort to make Terry notice her ample cleavage. "Looks like I'm all tapped out," she said, recapturing his attention away from her breasts.

"No cash, no product," Terry spoke robotically.

"Well, I was hoping maybe we could trade a favor for a favor," she replied with a devilish grin, licking her lips. Small traces of her prior beauty lingered but were definitely fading.

"No can do, sweetie. I'm on a mission right now," Terry said while fishing for another cigarette.

"Well, you lost!" Roxy capped as she turned to walk off. She hiked up her PINK sweatpants in one swift pull, playing the only card she had left. It was a very desperate move, but it had yet to fail her.

As Roxy slowly walked away, Terry couldn't help but look at the fabulous sight in front of him. The way Roxy's ass jiggled within the fabric of her sweats made him sweat. With every short, calculated step she took, something stirred within him, something he'd never quite had the chance to act on… Lust!

Inhaling the cancerous menthol, Terry said, "What did you have in mind?" loud enough for her to hear before she was too far.

Roxy smiled triumphantly before she turned around. She knew she had him right where she wanted him. The ass card worked every time on everyone. "You're the man on a mission, so uh, you tell me." She laid her game on thick as her thighs were.

Terry scanned the parking lot, the man he was waiting on still hadn't arrived, so he figured he had time to treat himself. "Well, there is something you could do for me," he said as his hand dragged slightly from his pocket, over the growing bulge in his 501's.

Expertly catching his drift, Roxy asked knowingly, "What's in it for me?"

Reaching into the front pocket of his oversized FCK PRISON hoodie, Terry produced a fresh ball of uncut meth. Bringing it into Roxy's view, her eyes danced with excitement, her heart skipped beats and her mouth salivated, anticipating the many highs to come off a score that size. At that moment she would have sold her soul for that sack. Should Terry ask anything less than that was no big deal, she thought.

"Show me the way," she said with a smirk.

"Gladly," Terry replied and took her hand in his.

With no specific destination in mind, Terry and Roxy rounded the building in search of a secluded area to perform their deed. Initially, contact with Roxy wasn't a part of Terry's plan. But, as the opportunity arose, he figured he could use her services in the long haul of his mission. In order for Roxy to be under his control fully though, he had to make a power move.

Stemming from his own past traumatic sexual experiences, Terry equated power with sex. Long ago, he had his power stripped from him and he had every intention to get it back.

Soon, they found a decent duck-off spot between two nearby buildings, camouflaged by a few army-green electric generators. Settling into the untraveled area, Roxy got comfortable and abruptly took control, figuring she knew exactly what the boy fifteen years her junior wanted.

She pushed Terry into a sitting position atop a generator, working to free his dick from the cover of his heavily creased jeans. In her mind, the faster she could make him cum, the faster she could take her trip to the moon.

When Terry's dick popped into view, Roxy was more than surprised with what the young boy had to offer. He was no Mandingo, but he was sure to reach depths within her that hadn't been explored in a few weeks.

Like she'd done so many times before, Roxy lowered her juicy mouth over the dick in front of her, taking it to the back of her throat with little effort.

Terry relaxed and watched on in awe, enjoying the sight of his very first blow job. The feeling was great, but not the sensation he craved. It wouldn't satisfy the feeling of power he so desperately sought. Still, for the hell of it, he let her work a minute or two longer.

"This feels great, but I had something a lil different in

mind," Terry said, pulling himself from her mouth, causing a popping noise when her oral fluids ran down the length of his stiffness.

He pulled Roxy to her feet and motioned for her to bend over the generator where he'd just sat. She followed his instructions and her ass went up in the air like two well-rounded mountains, making his dick throb harder.

Roxy looked back over her shoulder and said, "Ooh, a man that likes to get straight to the point, huh?"

Terry didn't reply, only continued through his progressions. Slowly, he pulled down her skin-hugging sweatpants, baring her porn star-like ass cheeks and a neatly trimmed pussy that glistened in the rays of morning sunlight.

Roxy took smooth deep breaths, waiting for Terry to impale her with his bulbous dick head and she spread her pussy lips wide for him in hopes of making the initial penetration easier. Standing directly behind her, Terry grabbed his member from the root and dragged it from the top of her clit back up to her opening, coating himself with extra juices before he dared enter her body.

Then, he spread her luscious cheeks and spit a string of slick saliva onto the muscular ring of her crimped asshole. Before Roxy could gather insight on his anal intentions, Terry thrust himself balls deep into her rarely entered rear passage. A mixture of both pain and pleasure overwhelmed her as he suddenly bombarded her tightest canal, stretching her beyond total comfort.

Holding the curve of her hips, Terry pumped away feverishly, his dick flying rapidly in and out of her like a piston. In short, he was giving Roxy the business for the agreed dope.

Roxy was caught completely off guard and was upset at first by Terry's actions. Her body's senses danced between euphoria and flares of agony with each stroke she faded. Remembering the size of that dope Terry had, magically, all the negative thoughts she had along with the pain disappeared. She figured if she could receive that kind of compensation from simply enduring the trauma of Terry's back-door assault, then fuck it! Might as well enjoy the encounter and have the best of both worlds. Moaning to show her conscience now, Roxy began throwing her ass back in a smooth clap.

Images of his own abuse flooded the forefront of his brain, fueling the powerful strokes Terry enforced on Roxy. He felt like a man now that he wasn't on the receiving end of this anal escapade. A few minutes passed before Terry got weak at the knees, grunted and his body spasmed, signaling the release of his seed, deep within Roxy's bowels. He felt accomplished and satisfied.

As Terry withdrew himself from Roxy's ever-tight grip, he could already feel the boost in his ego. Now he was even more ready to continue his plan and hopefully, with Roxy as his unknowing accomplice, he could execute it to the "T."

Terry and Roxy fixed their clothes and began to walk back to the spot where they originally had met.

"So, you held up your end of this deal and I appreciate that, but before I give you all of what I promised, I need one more small favor," Terry informed Roxy.

A look of complete disgust graded her face as she listened to his statement. Immediately, Roxy felt played and regretted not demanding her drugs upfront this time because she knew better. She'd been gamed out of her pants before, but because she assumed Terry was young and gullible, she thought payment wouldn't be an issue. She actually thought she'd be able to finesse more than agreed out of him.

As if Terry could read her mind, he continued. "You know who Jax is, right?

"Yeah, I mean, who doesn't?" She frowned. "What does he have to do with our deal?"

"Everything." Terry's face was serious. "Look, I'ma give you half now," he said, splitting the dope, "and I need you to come up to me and get this other half when you see that nigga pull up."

His suspicious request made Roxy second guess the entire deal, but she couldn't walk away from practically free dope. "Why?" she asked, accepting the half he gave her.

"Because I need his attention," Terry answered.

Terry could tell Roxy was worried about the other half of her payment still, so he leaned to sweeten the deal. "Look, take this as collateral," he said, taking a bankroll from his pocket. "When you see that nigga, come up to me like you're tryna cop somethin' and I'll give you the other half. Just slip me a thousand or so back, so it all looks legit and you can keep the rest for your troubles." Terry gave a wink.

Roxy eyed Terry like he was bat shit crazy, but she didn't dare turn down the deal of a lifetime. *A few G's and an ounce of Lubbock's finest was well worth the sore asshole I'm sporting, and whatever else came with it,* she thought.

"I think I like you already, Mr. Man," Roxy purred as she stuffed her rewards in the canyon of her cleavage.

"Just do me this favor and when I need you again, I know where to find you, we'll work something out," Terry suggested.

"Anytime." Roxy turned to make her way.

"Cool," Terry replied, then sparked another Newport.

———

A tad bit after 8:00 am, Jax pulled up in his 2020 Rolls Royce Wraith and parked in his designated spot. He was unusually agitated because he planned on coming to the studio at 10:00, but an early morning phone call changed that. His front desk representative, Lakesha, called him complaining about a lot of foot traffic and obvious drug transactions going on in front of the building. Lakesha knew Jax didn't deal with cops period, so she called to wake him up with the news, since neither Greedy or D. Lee had answered her call.

As Jax got out of his car and strode toward the studio doors, he caught the ass end of a clear drug deal between a woman with a big ole booty and some young punk in a hoodie.

He shook his head, unsure if he was upset or intrigued by the nerve of the dude. Jax wasn't egotistical, but he knew everyone in the city knew how he was built. So for someone to blatantly bring unwanted attention to his place of business was more than just disrespectful, it was utterly absurd. Instead of flying off the hinges and handling the situation recklessly, Jax approached the youngin' with an open mind.

"Say... look out, lil homie, wassup? What you got goin' on out here?" Jax's tone was even.

"Shit, nigga, what it look like? I'm tryna get my funds up like everybody should," Terry capped, stuffing the cash he got back from Roxy in his pocket.

Jax laughed, "Haha, I feel that shit. But, honestly though, you're going about it the wrong way."

"How you figure that?" Terry shot back. "You must not know who I am huh, youngsta?"

"From what I see, you just another nigga out here," Terry spoke down, intentionally trying to shoot daggers through Jax's ego.

"Ha, so I take it you don't... Well, I'm Jax, and this here is my shit." He pointed to the studio, then rubbed his hands together like Birdman for dramatic emphasis before continuing. "This my property you on as you say, 'tryna get your funds up' and I don't remember being cut in on shit or giving a nigga the go ahead to make my spot hot. So tell me, can you see the problem here?" Jax asked with a slight elevation of his voice.

"Damn, my bad, big homie, I had no idea." Terry feigned ignorance. "I thought you were just some random nigga tryna knock my hustle. But shit, I see I'm in the wrong and though I don't know you personally, I done heard about you. I got way too much respect for your gangsta to keep goin' against the grain. So with that being said, I'ma gone move around." Terry turned to walk away.

Jax stood puzzled, he half expected things to play way

differently with the young scraggly lookin' dude. "Aye, say, what's your name, kid?"

Terry spun on his heels, trying to think fast for a reply. There was a small chance Jax would recognize him by his real name and might even remember his face from his prior dealings with Lil Vicc, so he couldn't be truthful. He didn't want to risk Jax somehow making the connection so he gave a half-truth, something he'd remember and respond to. "Uh, T.J." He used his initials from his first and middle name.

"Okay. T.J., no disrespect to you and your hustle, but you don't really strike me as the dope boy type. So, let me ask you, why throw stones at the penitentiary? Selling drugs out in the open like it's legal for what? Better yet, why risk having a negative run in with me out here?"

"Well, just keeping it real with you, I mean all the way, 'IK', this is the only option I have. I come from less than nothing, so shit I'm just tryna make a way out of now way." Terry played his role well.

"What you 'bout, like eighteen? And you sayin' it's all you know. Your only option? Nigga, you still got a long life ahead of you. School, jobs, love, family and plenty of opportunity. So why become another statistic?"

"Man, I'm nineteen years old, educated, but I'm a black male felon in the undercover racist ass city of Lubbock. I ain't got no family or any positive role models, so Jax, please tell me where in the fuck my opportunity lies?"

"So you tellin' me, you're all alone and don't have anybody?" Jax couldn't believe that.

"Not a soul," Terry assured.

"And I mean like, you don't have skills at anything? No work history?"

"Well, like ninety-nine percent of all project niggas, I got skills on the field and the court but shit, I'd never make it at some white man's university. I didn't even graduate. I've never had a real job, considering how much time I spent locked up in juvenile hall, TYC or the county jail. I got some skills on the mic too, but nowadays everybody wanna be a rap nigga, so the shit played out. Who am I to think I'm so special I'll be the next to make it? Nah, I'll just take my chances out here." Terry nodded towards the street.

Jax soaked in all of Terry's words before he replied, "So, you think you a fool on the mic, huh?"

"I mean, I like to think so. I know for a fact I'm at least better than half these young colorful hair ass niggas out!" Terry said with a big chest.

"Aight. Come with me then. We gone see 'bout that hot shit you talkin'. If you got somethin' kid, I'ma help you chase your dreams 'cause everyone deserves a shot. If not, I'm not sure where we will go from here, but one thang's fa sho', you gone quit sellin' that shit in front of my building," Jax said. "Now, c'mon."

As Terry fell in step behind Jax, all he could think about his plan was, *so far so good*, while he internally mugged the man in front him.

18

TAKE A RIDE WITH ME

"So this the lil nigga Kesha said turned the front of the studio into a million-dollar trap?" Stephen asked while giving Terry the once over.

Jax laughed, "Yeah, this my man's T.J. T.J., this here is Stephen, the heartbeat of Studio 806 and Hub City Records. Everything that happens here with any of our artist's music is cleared by this man first. You said you got somethin', well here's the best judge for that," Jax pointed.

"Oh shit, a new recruit, huh? Jax, you know I love talent, let me go on and put him in the booth and see wassup," Stephen spoke anxiously. Music was definitely his passion.

"Do y'all. I'm just a spectator," Jax approved.

With that, Stephen took the reins.

"So, T.J., tell me. What kind of artist are you?"

"How can I put it?" Terry thought it out. "I'ma a young nigga but I ain't really on that new wave mumble shit like my peers. I appreciate lyricism to the fullest. I ain't rappin' about shit I ain't even done or the stereotypical drugs, guns, money and bitches. I rap about real life. My life, my struggles and overall real shit," he stated further.

"You more of an up-beat, high tempo, 'in your face' type rapper, or more dialed back and mellow?" Stephen asked, steepling his fingers in thought.

"Uh, really I'm kinda versatile with it. Just depends on the vibe of the whole track. I can get rah-rah on some Boosie-type shit if I want, but honestly I'm more in my comfort zone on my Bryson Tiller sing-songish type shit. Most people would say I remind them of another MO3, 'cause I'm street with it and can actually harmonize a bit."

"Well, shit, I can't wait to hear this. What kinda beat you wanna do?"

"Let me get something I can lay a smooth hook and bridge on, but let it be a lil more aggressive with delivering the bars so it stands out. Not too much bass, but enough. Maybe like a trap soul vibe so I can say some deep shit," Terry hurled suggestions.

"Gimme ten to fifteen minutes and I'll have somethin' ready for you," Stephen said before going to work. He put on his headphones and scooted closer to the wide computer screens in front of him. He moved quickly, yet efficiently, creating a custom beat on what looked like some really complex software. In no time, he was nodding his head, smiling in wait of what was to come.

When he finished, he unplugged the headphones and the catchy, melodic tune flowed throughout the room. Immediately, Terry's eyes sang approval before his mouth could.

"Hell, yeah! I can fuck with that shit," he exclaimed.

"Go 'head and get in the booth. Get comfortable with the beat and let me know when to start from the top," Stephen ordered.

As Terry entered the dark recording booth, his heart sank to the soles of his feet. It was beating so hard he wondered if they could hear it on the other side of the Plexiglass window. He knew he had to come with it in order to carry out the depth of his real plans with ease. And just maybe he could make somethin' happen for himself with the music along the way.

Terry gave Stephen the "I'm ready" nod and in seconds, the original beat pumped into his headphones. He closed his eyes, took deeply measured breath and poured his heart into the track, showcasing his singing and rap talents.

———

Hook… (He harmonized skillfully)

I'm livin' in tha ghetto, you know how it go/Neva know when them folks is on tha way to kick yo' doe/Where niggas be hustlin', tryna stack money on the low/I wanna see thangs that I ain't never seen before/But I'm livin' in tha ghetto/In tha ghetto/In tha ghetto/Oh livin' in that ghetto

Verse 1, (He rapped aggressively)

Man, I done seen a lot of shit/Comin' from a place where most niggas ain't got a pot to piss/Tha 'Ghetto', made a man outta me/Cause out here in these streets it's so amazing to see/Most of these fuck niggas ain't really who they claimin' to be/Through the struggle/Had to hustle to make ends meet/Wit all the troubles stood tall on my own two feet/From the ghetto up a level one day I'll be/One thang I guarantee is I won't wait forever to see/Cause I'm...

Bridge, (He sang smooth)

... livin' in tha ghetto and sometimes it got rough/Neva had it all but I always had enough/Tha pain neva ends but ya' gotta be tough/When ya' livin' in tha ghetto/In that ghetto/In that ghetto/oh livin' in tha ghetto...

Verse 2, (He vibed)

Niggas die on tha streets/You will get murdered fuckin' wit my family/that's on my brotha' my nigga may he rest in peace/I...

Suddenly, the beat died out. Stephen had heard enough to pass judgement.

Terry stepped back from the smoking mic and finally opened his eyes. Four astonished eyes stared his way.

Right after the beat dropped and the bass began its thud, Greedy and D. Lee stumbled into the room high as hell and full of that drank. They were present to witness the beginning of something great! Out of all the local talent on the Hub City Records roster, no one was coming that hard.

Stephen pressed a button on the control panel and said something over the mic into Terry's headphones. Terry came out the booth shortly afterward to join the congregation now surrounding the computer system.

"Yo', lil nigga tell me you wrote that?" Stephen had to know.

"Nah. Shit, I just put some thoughts together that I've been havin' 'bout life lately. What y'all think?" Terry asked with hope shining in his eyes.

"Man, I ain't even gone lie, lil bro," Stephen paused for effect. Meanwhile, Terry studied Jax's, Greedy's and D. Lee's motionless faces for an early answer. He couldn't gather one and hung his head low.

"That was some heat you dropped in there, kid! I mean, if that's the kinda shit you spittin on tha fly… shit, they better keep you away from a pen. No doubt, you got potential." Stephen gave credit where it was due.

"Damn, forreal? Don't be gassin' me up!" Terry squealed like a teen girl getting acknowledged by her celebrity crush.

"No bullshit! If I add a few effects to your hook and dub it, throw in more hi-hats with the verse and sprinkle in some fitting ad-libs, I personally think you have a radio hit. Local, at least, but who knows. It's gone be hard though, especially if that second verse some heat too," Stephen pumped.

Before Terry could gauge Stephen's seriousness, Jax cut in. "Stephen, I need you to make that happen, cause it looks like we've got ourselves a new addition to the team. That is, if you're in, right? I mean, you are in, right?" He stretched his hand out for Terry to seal a verbal contract.

For a brief second, Terry let the thoughts of money, power and fame that came with the rap game consume him, before he remembered the real reason he was in Jax's presence. With that, he shook on the deal.

"Good," Jax said with a smile. "T.J., come take a ride with me. We've got more to discuss."

———

As D. Lee steered Jax's elegant Wraith through the city, en route to 806 Customs, Greedy sat shotgun rolling a blunt. Terry and Jax lounged in the spacious backseat of the vehicle like mafia bosses.

Jax's right-hand men fired question after question to the youngsta and right away they could see why Jax took a liking to him so quickly.

D. Lee and Greedy had grown to be very protective of their friend Jax and always felt compelled to do a thorough critique of any new faces trying to penetrate the folds of their crew. This happened regardless if the venture was legal or illegal, but especially illegal.

Giving Terry the benefit of doubt about who he said he was and what he was saying he was about, D. Lee said, "Aight, Lil T.J. I fucks wit you. If my boss sees potential in you, then that really means something. Don't fuck it up." Greedy nodded in agreement.

"Don't start with that boss shit!" Jax said seriously, "we all equals 'round here, so long as you pull your weight."

"I fucks wit y'all too! Man, you niggas is like legends. I hope to learn a lot from each of you," Terry buttered their bread.

"Keep ya' eyes open and I'm sure you will," Greedy

spoke lightheartedly while putting fire on one end of the freshly rolled blunt.

"So wassup, Jax? Think we ought to invite the lil nigga to the party tonight, or nah?" D. Lee asked.

"What party?" Jax was perplexed.

"Tonight at Snows, we're having a celebration for 3BG's successful tour and return home," D. Lee reminded.

Damn, Jax thought internally. With all the bullshit happening recently, he'd fucked around and let the party he suggested they have, slip his mind. "Yeah, I don't see why not. It'll be a good way to introduce him to some of the other artists on the label anyway. But tell me, why we are having the party at Snows again?" Jax asked quizzically

"Simple. They got the livest drink specials. We can smoke in that muthafucka and besides that, we gotta handle that business wit Tony anyway. You said it would be killing two birds with one stone, remember?" Greedy threw in and exhaled a thick train of smoke.

Jax was forgetting a lot lately. "What time does it start again?"

"At 10:00," D. Lee answered and switched lanes.

"Right, well make sure we get Tony straight first. "

Terry was making mental notes of his plot around the 10:00 pm timeframe when Jax's question snapped his train of thought.

"So wassup, youngsta, you in?"

"Wouldn't miss it," Terry replied casually.

"We here… Boss," D. Lee laughed and watched Jax's reaction in the rear view mirror.

"Aight, drop us off around back. We will see y'all

tonight. And you niggas bet not scratch my shit," Jax said with raw sarcasm to his homies before he and Terry exited.

———

"Wassup? What we doin' here?" Terry asked as he looked around at all of the custom vehicles, scattered parts, tools and oil stains.

"We 'bout to pick up one of my new toys and holla at one of my niggas real quick. Then I'ma take you wherever you need to go so you can get ready for tonight."

"Aight," Terry nodded.

Jax and Terry maneuvered through all the clutter and ducked under the half-open garage door. Finally, they stopped walking once they reached a pair of legs, sticking out from underneath one of the world's most expensive sports cars.

Clumsily, Terry accidentally kicked the corner of a metal toolbox, making it tilt then fall, causing a sudden crash. Before Jax could voice their arrival more appropriately, the man under the vehicle rolled out in a flash with something ugly in his right hand and a deadly gleam in his eyes. He looked ready to do damage until he seemed to recognize one of the faces in front of him.

"Damn, Cuz! You almost made me smoke yo' goofy ass," the man said as he tucked away the golden .50 cal Desert Eagle into the chambers of his soiled coveralls. "It's 'bout time you made it out here. Shit, I almost thought you was gone let me keep this bitch all to myself," he said to Jax, but eyed Terry. The name tag on his chest read, "Hot Boi."

Jax reached out and locked C's with the man. "My fault, Cuz. I been hella busy with shit these past few days. Everything's been crazy," Jax said honestly.

"So I've heard. Yo gon' be straight?"

"Minor setbacks. You know how the game go," Jax sounded full of street wisdom.

"Indeed I do."

Hot Boi may have looked like your ordinary mechanic, but to those that knew his true character, knew much more lurked beneath his surface. He was a dangerous man of many trades. Hot Boi had his hands in some of everything, from drugs to contract killing, running numbers, prostitution and his specialty, exotic firearms dealing. If anybody would understand what Jax was going through with Tuck's situation, Hot Boi would.

"Who's our friend?" Hot Boi nodded towards Terry. He was usually suspicious of new faces and rightfully so, considering the amount of dirt he did. But, since Jax brought him in, he figured he was solid.

"This my lil nigga, T.J. He one of the new artists on my label and maybe my new protege."

Protege? Terry thought. He was curious but kept silent as if he hadn't heard the comment.

"Oh, aight. I see." Hot Boi expected a different answer but respected the one he got. "S'up, youngsta? I'm Hot Boi." He extended a fist. "If you gon' be rollin' wit Jax I'm sure you'll be seeing a lot of me."

Terry looked at the extended fist and returned the dap. "Nice to meet ya," he said.

"So this my new baby, huh?" Jax openly admired the V12 beauty in front of him. It was a shiny, Nipsey blue

Bugatti Chiron, fresh off the press. Jax pondered the times he couldn't even afford to dream of a car that superb. Now, he could legally purchase multiple if he chose to do so.

"Yeah, that's it. I just finished the last of the customs you requested and I did a few extra. The blinging paint, plush cocaine white interior, upgraded sound system, secret compartments, run-flats and hell, I even armored this mu'fucka with bulletproof glass! Trust me when I say this bitch is lit. Now, the ticket will be a lil higher than we originally discussed but I know you and know you'd want the best," Hot Boi reasoned while he scrubbed the grit from his hands in a nearby work sink.

"Oh shit!" Jax turnt up. "So, you tellin' me, not only do I now have a Bugatti but I got a muthafuckin' bulletproof Bugatti!" he raved with excitement.

"On top of that, according to my source, this is the only Bugatti in West Texas," Hot Boi added to the hype.

"Man, I'm 'bout to fuck the game up wit this one! Shit, I'm ready to pull off in this bitch right now. I'm gone go in the office and settle my dues with Lisa, keep my lil homie entertained for a second," Jax threw over his shoulder before disappearing.

Seeing the look in Terry's eyes while he observed the car and the others around it, Hot Boi knew he had a fan. Eager to show off some of his other handiwork, he said, "You like guns, kid?"

"Yeah, who doesn't?" Terry replied. He was crouched down, staring at his reflection in the chrome rims of the Bugatti.

"Shit, niggas on the wrong end of them mu'fuckas,

that's who!" Hot Boi was both sarcastic and serious. "Follow me."

Somewhere at the back of the sizable garage along the dark gray walls, Hot Boi toyed with a keypad for a few seconds before the wall split in two with a low pressurized hiss, revealing some *Mission Impossible* type shit.

Rows upon rows of automatic pistols, sniper rifles, sub-machine guns, grenades, knives and a slew of other devices littered the wall under halos of bright fluorescent light. High priced scopes, suppressors, beams and extended mags of all sorts gracefully adorned the cache of weapons.

Terry couldn't believe his eyes. He was stunned and stood with his mouth agape for a moment.

"Let it sink in… Everyone usually does that when they first lay eyes on this treasure chest of mine," Hot Boi gloated.

Terry slowly paced up and down the stretch of the wall, examining every gun until his eye caught the one.

"Damn, I always wanted one of these right here," Terry stated, holding the onyx black HK MP5. The weapon was a real masterpiece fitted with a bushmaster scope, suppressor, fifty-round magazine and a camo shoulder strap.

"Is that so?" Hot Boi raised a brow.

"Hell, yeah! This hoe clean then a bitch."

"I tell you, what lil homie… come up with a stack and it's all ours. I could get 'bout fifteen hundred to two thousand for it on the streets. But, since Jax brung you here, you gotta be solid, so a G will do—"

Before Hot Boi could even finish his statement, Tery pulled out the remainder of money he had earlier that day from inside the pockets of the gym shorts he sported under his jeans. He quickly gave it to Hot Boi with no regrets.

"Damn, youngsta, you 'bout yo' business, huh?" Hot Boi complimented.

"Always," Terry replied. He then took off his oversized FCK PRISON hoodie and slid the camo shoulder strap around his torso, clasping the weapon like one of those baby carriers, before pulling the hoodie over his head again.

What Hot Boi didn't know was when he accepted the cash, he gave Terry the very instrument he needed to carry out the physical side of a plan already in motion.

"I should have known y'all would be back here playin' G.I. Joe," Jax joked once he finally found Hot Boi and Terry.

Hot Boi simply shrugged and hit the numbers on the keypad, closing the doors on his beloved arsenal.

"You got them keys ready for me?" Jax asked. He was more impatient than a kid waiting to open gifts on Christmas morning. But, for reasons any man or true car fan could understand.

"Here you go, Cuz. C-careful out there. Don't be gettin' no speedin' tickets and shit!" Hot Boi teased.

"Yeah, aight. C'mon T.J., we out!" Jax said as he caught the keys in the air.

Once behind the wheel, Jax inserted the high-tech key, turned over the ignition and lightly pressed the gas, making the beast roar to life. Like a mad man, he threw the gear shift in drive and floored the pedal, making the car's tires burn rubber and leave a tail of smoke behind.

All Hot Boi could do was laugh and really admire the life-style of his good friend. Far as he could see, Jax was livin' it up!

———

Flying down the Marsha Sharp Freeway, Jax and Terry were glued by G-Force to the racer style seats. They were enjoying the high speeds of their travel while the voice of Jaquille serenaded their ears through the crisp speakers. For a moment, Terry was having so much fun with the man in the driver's seat, he forgot how much he really hated him.

Suddenly, he wanted to pull the MP5 from under his hoodie and feed Jax the clip, but at the speeds they were going, shooting Jax now would surely cost him his life too. Plus, if he killed Jax before making him suffer more, that would be letting him off easy and there was no way possible that was happening, so he held his composure.

"Aye, T.J. I got one more stop to make. Should take no more than a few minutes, then I'ma drop you off, that's cool?"

"My nigga, I'm tryna stay in this car for as long as possible. Handle your business, fam!" Terry said with a well-practiced fake laugh.

———

Jax exited the freeway and pulled into a decent little neighborhood, tucked behind a park just off West 4th Street. He parked in front of what seemed to be a newly built brick home that had an old Honda Civic under the carport and a boy's BMX bike in the grass. He pulled out his iPhone X and typed feverishly into the screen.

Seconds later, the front door to the home opened and a short, thick, white woman came out. Terry noticed she was good looking in the face but could stand to shed a few pounds of baby weight. Still, the woman strutted over as if she were *America's Next Top Model*.

"I'll be just a minute," Jax said and hopped out.

The woman, now even prettier up close, stood just a few feet away from the seven-figure automobile, tapping her foot and showing visible signs of frustration. Out of sheer curiosity, Terry cracked his window a bit so he could hear their convo.

"Okay, Cori, I'm here. You got my attention now. What the fuck is so damn important you've been textin' and callin' me all damn morning? I swear, if it ain't got shit to do with Jr., me and you gone have an issue!" Jax spat.

"Uh, first of all, don't be yellin' at me, nigga, is you stupid or just crazy? Second, it is about your son! When are you gonna spend some quality time with him, huh?" Cori snaked her neck in a way that betrayed her suburban upbringing.

"Woman, you must be the one that's crazy. Hell you talkin' 'bout? I spend time with my son every week on the days I was given right to by the judge and I ain't ever missed a day. So what the fuck type of shit you on? You comin' at me like I'm some kind of dead beat and you know better than that!" Jax fumed.

"Could've fuckin' fooled me!" Cori spewed venomously.

"Bit —" Jax caught the word before he let it slip. Every

part of him wanted to grab Cori and choke her out, but he refrained. "You so fulla shit! The only times you try to give me more time with Jr. is when it's beneficial for you. So, let me guess, you must be tryna skip town with that lil weak ass nigga you wit for the weekend or something like that?" Jax hit the nail on the head.

"Kenny is not weak. He's more of a man to me then you—" Cori tried to defend, but Jax cut her off.

"Honestly, I don't give a damn. But I see I was right in my assumption. Anyway, my time with Jr. starts tomorrow night and that's when I'll be by to get him. Unlike you, I actually have a business to tend to that allows me to financially support my child. So, I'll pick him up when I'm not workin', as I do faithfully, every fuckin' week!" Jax went off.

"You're just selfish and hate to see me happy!" Cori yelled like a real psych patient.

"Actually, I've never been selfish! True enough though, I don't give a fuck about your happiness 'cause that ain't my job no more. I only care for Jr.'s. I'm doing my duty as a father and much more. Let's not forget I bought you this muthafuckin house and I've been payin' the bills 'round this bitch since your lazy ass decided to quit your job. So don't you dare come at me sideways!" Jax was trying to take it easy, but Cori was really getting under his skin.

"Nigga, you ain't doin' shit," Cori said, sounding so stubborn and ungrateful. "The little money you give me and this little ass house ain't shit compared to how you're livin' on the other side of town in that big ass mansion. You don't care 'bout Jr., or else we'd be right there with you, be real!

I see you rollin' 'round here all in exotic cars while you got your son stuck in a damn Honda!" Cori folded her arms.

All Jax could do to keep from kicking Cori's ungrateful ass was laugh. He always knew she wasn't 'bout shit, but at that moment she was out of control.

"Wow, I always knew you were fucked up in the head... but damn, not this bad. Seems to me like you're actually the one who don't care about Jr. . You acting like this because you want to go on a trip with your lil boyfriend and you have to wait because you have motherly responsibilities! Sad part is, neither you nor Kenny got any money, so this trip most likely would have been on my dime. Your triflin' ass using my son's money on God knows what! Look, Cori, I'ma tell you like this," Jax got real serious. "The only fuckin' reason I haven't took you back to court again and fought for full custody which I know I could get now, is 'cause Jr. still loves your punk ass and I don't want to hurt my baby boy. I swear to God though, you keep up with this bullshit and this house gone seem real big with only you in it." Jax let the threat hang in the air a second before he returned to his car and smashed off.

———

"Not tryna get all up in your business, big homie, but shit looked a lil heated back there. You good?" Terry questioned.

"Yeah, I'm good. Where you need to go now?" Jax changed subjects.

"Uh... Uh," Terry stumbled to find a fitting answer. He

knew if he told Jax Lil Vicc's address, shit would hit the fan. "Um, drop me off on the east side in the projects."

"Bet that. Shit, you gone be ready for tonight?"

"Yeah, I'll be through like 10:30 or so. I gotta go handle a few things first, but trust, I'll be there."

"Aight then, check it. Monday we gone get together with my lawyers, draw up some contracts and see if we can't ink you an official deal. I told you if you had some talent, I was gonna help you pursue your dreams and I meant that. So be on your best shit and don't let me down," Jax said.

"Jax, I really appreciate the opportunity. Shit like this don't happen every day. One thing I can say is I'ma definitely surprise you. My word on that!" Terry said to Jax, meaning something totally different than what Jax assumed.

19

A SHOOTING AT SNOW CITY

SNOW CITY WASN'T the most extravagant night spot in Lubbock. It wasn't the biggest place or the most expensive either, but it held a solid reputation for being a neutral haven for any and all gangs, races and financial classes. Snow City conducted good business and boasted great drink specials, a weed friendly atmosphere and a drama free environment that made the place a hit with all the Lubbock locals. Especially natives of the "East Side," where the club was located.

The owner of Snow City was a thorough street nigga named Tony Snow. Tony was, no doubt, a gangsta in the city and his name held a great deal of weight. He and Jax went to the same schools growing up and maintained cordial friendships, but mostly traveled two different paths those days.

Back then, Jax wanted to be the next NFL superstar and Tony wanted to be the black *Scarface*. When Jax plugged into the drug trade years later, it was Tuck who reunited the two men on street business and the duo had been making lots of money together ever since.

———

At approximately 9:30 pm, Terry positioned himself on the rusty, steel ladder attached to the side of Snow City's building and climbed onto the roof with his new MP5, hanging from a shoulder strap. He had been waiting all day since Jax dropped him off that morning for this moment and now his nerves were getting the best of him.

His palms felt damp and his forehead and armpits began to sweat profusely. Terry had done some G-shit in his young life, but never anything like what he was 'bout to do. As the saying goes though, "There's a first time for everything."

As Terry crouched behind the cover of the Snow City "Snowflake" sign, he witnessed car after car arrive in the warped parking lot. Some of the faces he'd seen before and some he hadn't, but he studied each of them intently as they paraded into the club.

Looking through the lens of his BushMaster Scope, Terry's heart started to beat faster than normal, when the trio he awaited pulled up in in a stretch Hummer limo. The chauffeur parked smoothly, got out and proceeded to open the rear right door for the occupants. Out stepped Greedy and D. Lee, draped and dripped in their finest designer and jewels, accented by two beautiful women on their arms.

Jax followed up behind them, holding a large gift bag in one hand which contained a present for each member of 3BG, and a Brooks Brothers duffle bag in the other.

Terry surveyed the group from his sniper's perch as they all approached the unsecured entrance to the club, while his moist index finger lightly caressed the MP5's hair trigger. Luck that night was on his side somehow, security was not present for this private party. A party that would house many people of financial, cultural and street significance for the night.

Terry, as nervous as he was, was about to open fire prematurely, before he froze upon hearing Jax's command to D. Lee and Greedy.

"Aye, y'all go 'head and take this duffle and get Tony all squared away. Tell that nigga I put five extra on top for hosting tonight's event. Then bring the money back out to the limo and leave it with the driver. Hurry up though so we can enjoy the party. Shit, as hard as we work, we got just as much reason for celebration as 3BG does. Now, ladies..." Jax raised his elbows and the two beauties interlocked their arms in his and walked gracefully inside.

Terry held his breath but smiled internally, because things had gotten a lot sweeter than he expected. He was smart enough to know anybody Jax did business with had to be comin' correct with the cash. So, if he waited a bit longer, he might be able to remove another piece in this twisted chess game.

Thirty-five minutes later, Greedy and D. Lee exited the front entrance to Snow City carrying an identical Brooks Brothers duffle bag to the one they arrived with. It appeared just as heavy, if not heavier.

It wasn't late yet, but the party was in full swing by now and the charming tones of BANK$ could be heard all the way in the parking lot, as he flowed through the state-of-the-art sound system.

When Greedy and D. Lee's feet touched the uneven pavement outside the building, they stood motionless for a few breaths, scanning the parking lot cautiously. They looked over the sea of expensive vehicles in search of the limo and driver. Much to their dismay, the chauffeur parked in the only space large enough to accommodate the limo about a hundred yards away. Before the two close friends could make the journey to the limo, a sudden noise caught their attention, only they couldn't pin the location.

"Wht!" Terry whistled again in a mocking manner. "Aye, up here!" he screamed, gathering their undivided attention.

"Lil T.J., the fuck ya doin' up there?" D. Lee questioned.

"Something I've been waiting to do a long time!" T.J. replied with an evil grin as he raised the MP5 and fired.

Greedy instantly realized the young nigga wasn't playing any games and was in fact dead serious on his intent. His refined killer instincts kicked in as he attempted to draw his twin Glock .40's. But he was nowhere near as fast as the speeding bullets fired from the automatic weapon.

"Fhtttttttt - Fhtttttttt," the MP5 made a deadly whisper, as metal leapt from the end of the gun's suppressor in rapid succession, only to find refuge in Greedy's flesh.

For a split second, D. Lee seemed to be cemented in place, forced to watch one of his best friends get savagely gunned down in the air of night. Since he, Greedy, and Jax got in the game, it was a cardinal rule to stay strapped at all times. In their eyes, it was a downright sin to be caught without it. That day, of all days, D. Lee was naked and it would cost him. Greedy was already dead so he knew there was no talking his way out of the situation at hand. So, he turned to do the only thing he could in hopes of living... Run!

Reverting back to his old high school football days, D. Lee tucked the duffle bag in his right arm like a football, turned on his heels and ran with the speed of a professional athlete. Even with his life on the line, his speed was tortoise-like compared to the MP5's 9mm slugs.

"Fhttttttt." The MP5 fired away and Terry cut D. Lee down like a tree.

To ensure himself that he'd finished the job, Terry did a video game like jump onto the roof of a brand-new black Beamer, causing the roof to sink in a little. But that didn't matter, he was like a predator in pursuit of wounded prey.

Reaching the ground, he approached D. Lee swiftly. The man was in bad shape, but miraculously still alive, even after the acceptance of ten lead offerings. He crawled miserably over the gravel covered parking lot, leaving a trail of blood in his wake. Terry watched on in silence, enjoying the sight of D. Lee's suffering.

He kicked D. Lee in his ribs, making him roll over on his back and sense movement. With a foot now on his chest, D. Lee looked up into the eyes of his potential killer while blood poured from his wounds and mouth.

"Why are you doing this?" D. Lee managed the strength

to ask. The blood in his mouth was threatening to choke and kill him before Terry could.

Simply because he could, Terry entertained the question and gave an answer. "Well, let's just say your loyalty lie with the wrong nigga. Don't take this personally. Blame it all on Jax!" he teased before a quick tap on the MP5's trigger sent five more bullets on a mission.

In just thirty-five silent shots, Terry changed the game and one family's life forever. He felt an immense wave of pleasure doing so. Quickly after his deadly deeds, Terry fled the scene, leaving D. Lee and Greedy holier than the church on Easter Sunday.

———

Terry ran non-stop and as fast as he could for two blocks while his adrenal glands kicked into overdrive. The double homicide he'd just pulled off went without a hitch and his once shattered ego was now mended. The only thing now that could elevate the blissful feeling surging through his veins, would be seeing the look on Jax's face when he stumbled upon the mess in Snow City's parking lot.

Terry ducked into a small alley not far from the crime scene, right behind a run-down apartment complex in "Parkway" everyone called the "PV's." He forced himself to calm down and fixed his appearance with a clean collared shirt and pants he'd hidden in the alley inside a throw-away bag prior to the shooting. Before leaving the alley, Terry unzipped the duffle bag he'd relieved D. Lee of and truly couldn't believe his eyes.

Never, ever had he seen so many dead presidents

staring back at him. The stolen money was a sight to see, but there was something else he longed to lay eyes on at the moment that was better than the visual of blue hundreds and red fifties. Without bothering to count the money, he placed the gun in the bag and tucked it safely behind a dumpster between the steel container and a leaning fence. Then to save face, he headed back to Snow City.

———

"Man, see here you go wit' dat bullshit again! Straight trippin'! That's why I don't eva take yo' muthafuckin' ass nowhere," Fudda Mayne fussed at his baby mama, as he ducked and dodged the physical assault she was dishing out to him.

"Yeah, whateva nigga. I ain't trippin', you the one that's trippin', you lyin' muthafucka! I know damn well what I just seen up in there. Fuck you and that *bitch!*" she yelled with emphasis on the bitch part, "think y'all slick... you still fuckin' her too?" she asked as her voice jumped between anger and heartbreak.

"You know damn well I ain't fuckin' that girl," Fudda lied. "How could I be, when I spend all my free time outside the studio with you?" he yelled, stepping out of the Snow City building. Fudda shook his head because not even thirty minutes into the party, Dezzy was acting a damn fool... as usual.

"I can't believe you would do me like this, nigga, I'm havin' yo baby!" she spat, trying to play mind games. Dezzy knew damn well the baby she was carrying wasn't Fudda's. It's just that Fudda Mayne was a budding hip-hop artist signed to one of the hottest labels in the game, so there was no way she was letting him slip away. Not a chance.

Dezzy continued to bicker and they were just a few paces away from Fudda's car when he couldn't hold his tongue any longer.

"Bitch… you must think you slick! I know your lil secret. Haha, everybody ain't yo' friend, believe that!" Fudda teased. "That baby ain't mine —" The sight of the damage on his Beamer caught his eyes. "That's my baby right there… Look at my roof. Oh shit, look. At. my. roof! See, niggas play too much!" Fudda seethed comically.

Deezy couldn't contain her laughter. She wasn't laughing at the damage itself, but rather Fudda's reaction to it. He sounded like Day-Day from *Next Friday*, spazzin' about his damn car roof. She was more than happy that the attention was no longer being aimed at her prior infidelities.

Fudda walked around the Beamer, trying to evaluate the damage to his prized possession when he discovered the massacre. Two men he actually had love for and looked up to, lay slain in a crimson river of blood. Without thinking, Fudd rushed to Greedy's body, which was the nearest to the car. When he searched for signs of a pulse and felt none, he screamed out to Dezzy, "Go get some help! Hurry! Get Jax!"

———

"Alright, alright, everybody gather 'round. First, I want to really thank each and every one that came out tonight, in support of 3BG and Hub City Records. I'd like to propose a toast—" Jax was in mid-speech before his words were cut by Deezy's paralyzing scream.

"Jax! Jax, hurry they got shot! Somebody shot 'em! They dead!" Deezy sobbed. "I think they're dead."

Not asking who, Jax shot off the stage, fearing the worst. In stride, he realized it'd been a little too long since he last saw Greedy and D. Lee. He ran faster, easily maneuvering through the small club as a group of partygoers followed.

When Jax made it to the parking lot, he held his breath until his eyes locked with Fudda's and he rushed over to him. Fudda was kneeling over Greedy's body crying silently. Jax didn't want to believe the sight of one of his niggas laying there lifeless. Frantically, he looked around hoping to see D. Lee somewhere, alive and well. His heart broke when his eyes landed on D. Lee's bullet-riddled body not far away.

Jax was overcome with dread and sorrow. The world seemed to be spinning out of control and he fought to come to grips with reality.

"Dezzy, Dezzy! What the fuck happened?" Jax yelled through tears.

"I-I don't know," Dezzy stepped forward from the crowd. "Me and Fudda came out and they were already laying there," She sniffled. Dezzy had no ties to Greedy, but she and D. Lee were a lot closer than people knew about. Real close.

The other party-goers, from the famous to irrelevant, all spread through the parking lot, being nosey and trying to get a glimpse of the victims. Some had enough sense to call an ambulance. Others recorded the tragic incident in hopes to gain likes or clout on Facebook and Instagram.

Knowing there was nothing Jax could do to save his friends gave Terry total satisfaction while he watched from behind the cover of a parked car. Once he finally thought Jax had momentarily suffered enough, he popped out and made his next move.

"Jax!" Terry yelled, running up to him, pretending to be out of breath.

"T.J., what the fu—" Jax stammered.

"Jax, listen! Them niggas ran that way," Terry pointed, "I saw the whole thang," he said truthfully. "C'mon, if you hurry we can catch 'em," he lied.

20

SOMEONE WILL PAY FOR THIS

IT'D BEEN EXACTLY seven days since the fatal shooting at Snow City and Jax was still far from his normal self. Just an hour prior to this moment, Jax and hundreds of other people gathered together at the Lubbock Cemetery to pay their final respects to the dearly departed, as D. Lee and Greedy were simultaneously lowered six feet into the womb of earth, marking the eternal resting place of their physical form. Jax couldn't bear the sight or shake the gut-wrenching pain in his heart.

The thought of D. Lee and Greedy rotting in the dirt, along with Tuck withering away in a cell somewhere for God knows how long didn't sit well with him. All the love and support shown by family, friends and fans at the funeral, coupled with the pastor's beautiful eulogies, made the entire process a bit easier to bear.

Jax sat between both of his friends' headstones, wallowing in the throes of sorrow. Indeed it was a tough loss and very uneasy to come to grips with their tragic demise too soon. Jax was grief-stricken and enraged. When he finally found the strength to rise to his feet, Jax made a solemn vow to his fallen comrades, "Someone will pay for this!"

"Come on, Jax, it's gone be aight, man. Stay strong! We got to get up outta here. We gone come back to visit once we find and deal with the niggas that put them here," Terry said out loud as he approached Jax, snapping him out of his daze.

"You right T.J." Jax wiped his eyes. "I'ma be back, my niggas. 'Cause standin' here cryin' and shit ain't gone help me find the muthafuckas that did this! I love y'all. Make sure y'all watch over me," Jax said to the headstones.

"So now what?" Terry asked once they were in the back of the limo, unaccompanied.

"Now we wait on that info, 'cause somebody knows somethin'. I got that hundred-thousand-dollar-reward out for any information that's gone lead me to them fuck niggas! Everybody actin' all tight-lipped right now, like nobody knows shit, but trust me when I say for a hundred-K, the streets gonna start talkin' and all I need is a whisper."

"Well, big homie, I just want you to know I'm with you, all the way. I'm with whateva, howeva! Shit, since we met you been helpin' me chase my dreams, so in return I'ma help you catch these demons," Terry faked his sincerity with ease.

"I appreciate you, Lil T.J. Means a lot. Loyalty will get you a very long way with me. Keep that in mind."

"Always," Terry replied simply.

"Well, honestly, I'm not in much of a mood for food but

my mom and aunts are cooking. You know niggas always cook after funerals, weddings, holidays and all that shit. So I gotta stop by. You hungry?" Jax offered.

Terry rubbed his stomach and quickly replied, "Yeah, I could eat." True enough, he was starved, but he secretly was more interested in tagging along for recon purposes and gaining more intel on Jax's family.

Just as Terry planned, he and Jax became close in a very short time span. That fatal night at Snow's, Terry and Jax ran off into the night chasing ghosts. Terry had told Jax he was just walking up to the club when he saw two niggas in dark clothing and ski-masks approach Greedy and D. Lee from behind and open fire. He said they had automatic weapons, equipped with silencers and once they eliminated their targets, they fled on foot, running west down Parkway Drive before disappearing into a thick wooded area with the duffle bag in tow.

Jax and Terry ran around aimlessly for a while in the general direction Terry gave, only to come up empty handed and heavy hearted. Jax was upset that he couldn't avenge his homies right then and there, but he swore he'd make things right.

As part of his plan, Terry offered his assistance and at first Jax was a bit skeptical, but Terry seemed genuine in his ways, even though he barely knew Greedy or D. Lee. Since Jax no longer had anyone to help with his street affairs and shit was getting hectic, he made a hasty decision. Against his better judgment, Jax brought Terry up to speed on his operations, intending to groom his new protege. He treated Terry just like one of his late, day-ones.

21

FAMILY INTEL

TERRY TOOK in every detail of Mecia's marvelous home, as he and Jax entered the door. Mecia was Jax's mother, one of the wealthiest men in Lubbock, but she still resided in the midst of a semi-impoverished neighborhood. Not because she had to but simply by choice.

The old home she occupied had been in the family for generations and with any luck, it would stand for generations to come. In her heart, it held a significant sentimental value. Jax's great-grandparents, Marshall and Ella Mae Cook, worked their fingers to the bone, day in and day out to purchase the home in the late fifties. They would turn over in their graves if another family was to ever lay claim to it. Knowing that, Mecia refused to move and abandoned the only true home she'd ever known.

Although Jax stressed his opinion of Mecia moving into a better neighborhood with nicer homes plenty of times, often with valid reasoning, she decided against his wishes time after time. But she did make the most Jax's idle threats, by simply allowing Jax to have the house completely renovated. After adding on a bit to the rear of the home, re-painting, adjusting the front and backyard landscape, updating appliances, decor and home furnishings, the house stuck out like a sore thumb in the neighborhood.

Even though he'd only been inside the home for mere seconds, Terry was able to diagnose that the house truly felt like a home, a place filled with so much love, laughs, and memories. Instantly, he became even more envious of Jax, because he never had a chance to experience a loving home as a child. The resentment within him grew with every step down the main hallway, as he was greeted by all the posted family photos, certificates, awards and scholastic accolades. Terry felt in his heart it was his sole purpose in life to bring this family down a notch and so far he was off to a very good start and no one knew a thing. Mentally, he gave himself a pat on the back.

The house was mostly quiet, save for a few faint voices coming from the kitchen. Jax and Terry drew near the voices and were surprised to see five beautiful women gracefully and skillfully preparing a delicious smelling meal. Two of the three women seemed to be in a totally different headspace than the others, but Terry understood why. Losing a child could take a toll on one's heart in a major way.

In a stellar sixth sense that only mothers seem to possess, Mecia felt a presence and turned accordingly to speak. "Hey, Son. Barely heard you come in. Go on to the table and have a seat with Marcus, the food is almost ready." Her tone was so sweet and loving it made Terry feel warm and welcome even though she hadn't yet acknowledged his presence.

Marcus' undivided attention was afforded to the ESPN app on his phone until he heard the approaching footsteps. When he turned and saw Jax, he rose to hug his older brother. "Jax, you okay, big bro?"

"To be honest, bro, I'm not. But I will be when I get my revenge."

"My homie from around the corner says he heard you got a huge reward out. Any luck with some info?"

"Nah, not yet, but I'ma hear somethin' soon. I can feel it!" Jax said confidently.

"Bro, you know if you ever need me, I'll help in any way I can. D. Lee and Greedy were like my big brothers too! Shit, I miss 'em already," Marcus admitted.

"Yeah, I know, lil bro. But check it, the only way you can help me is by staying out the way. You done made it this far without getting your nose dirty and I plan to keep it that way," Jax scolded lightly.

Marcus hated that Jax still treated him like a kid sometimes, but he was smart enough to understand it was for his own good. "So, who's this?" He changed the subject. He gave Terry a glance.

"This is T.J., he's a new friend of mine and also one of my new artists," Jax gave his answer as a way of introduction.

Marcus and Terry spoke and shook hands respectfully, but deep down, Marcus was suspicious of Terry and couldn't detect why. He just seemed off. Especially in close comparison to the late Greedy and D. Lee.

"Ma told me this is gonna be one of your last weekends at home. You sure you're ready to leave the nest?" Jax asked.

"Hell yeah, I'm ready!" Marcus exclaimed. "I mean, don't get me wrong. I love Ma and being around, but I'm ready to experience more in life, even if it's just living in a dorm a few miles away from home... full of coeds!" Marcus winked.

"I feel that, lil bro. So, when are you leavin'?"

"Soon! I already got everything packed."

"Damn, haha. I guess you are ready!" Jax laughed. "Well I'm sure you know to call me if you need anything. I won't be far. "

"That's overstood!"

As Jax and Marcus continued small talk about Marcus' role in the upcoming season at Tech, Terry was rapidly plotting in his head on how to make sure Marcus never made it to campus. He simply couldn't allow that!

After what seemed like an eternity, Mecia, Ke, Kam, D. Lee's mother Denise and Greedy's mother Janet came out of the kitchen, carrying steaming pots and pans of seasoned vegetable and savory meats. The sensational aroma of secret family recipes filled the air and consequently made Terry's stomach rumble.

Everyone sat comfortably at the eight-person dining table and said a memorable grace after plates were filled. Unlike the rest of the table, Jax was still unable to gain an appetite and Denise noticed.

"Jax, you don't look so good, son," she said so tenderly.

"'Cause I'm not. Ms. Denise, I can't lie, this loss really hurt me. I swear, I never expected anything like this to happen. I feel completely lost and helpless. I hate that I can't do anything to bring them back and I hate the nigga that took my brothers away!" Jax said what was on his heart.

Beneath his straight face, Terry was smiling.

"Jax, baby, you can't beat yourself up over this. Yes, it is very painful for everyone but I believe God does everything for a reason. We may not agree or understand some-things, but as followers of our savior, we must accept the hand he deals to us," Ms. Janet chimed in with painful acceptance.

Mecia became close friends with Denise and Janet through the church. The friendship their sons maintained only made it easier for them to form a solid bond. When Mecia received the news of Greedy and D. Lee's deaths, she felt as though she'd also lost a child. Better yet, two! In order to help her friends through this unspeakable tragedy, she had to stay strong.

"Now son, we heard about the reward offer you have out and we think it's good you're trying to get justice for D. Lee and Greedy. But, please son, don't do anything crazy. Let the police do their job," Mecia pleaded. She was trying to be strong for Denise and Janet considering their loss, but she knew if the shoe were on the other foot, she'd lose her mind!

"Ma, you know I love you and I have much love and respect for Ms. Denise and Ms. Janet as well. But I can't make any promises. Y'all know just like I know the police don't care about no niggas gettin' gunned down in the ghetto. Seems to me like the only people who care are in this room. I'ma make sure somebody pays for this!" Jax declared.

"Son, I know you're hurt and you need to give yourself time to heal. Don't do anything irrational, this family has already been through enough and my heart can't take much more," Mecia applied her guilt trip, both hands on her chest.

Without further rebellion, Jax agreed to chill. The last thing he needed was to be the cause of his mother's heart failure.

"Thank you, son. I love you so much. Now, I have two questions," Mecia said between bites.

"I love you too, Ma. Okay, now shoot."

"Will you go up to the pharmacy and pick up my script tomorrow? I can't 'cause of a few scheduled church affairs, Ke will be busy with school stuff and Kam has studio sessions all day."

"Yeah Ma, no problem. I'll make sure to do that for you."

"And my other question is, who is this handsome young man you brung in? I don't believe we've met."

"Oh, sorry 'bout that, y'all. Just been a lot going on. This is T.J. T.J. this is my mom Mecia, you met Marcus, these are my sisters Kam and Ke," Jax pointed to everyone, "and these women here are like my aunts, Denise and Janet."

"Uh, hello to you all. Let me say it was not my intention to be rude and not introduce myself. It's just under the circumstances of this dinner, I wanted to be respectful and not rub anyone the wrong way," Terry spoke so properly Jax had to look at him twice to see if he changed. "Oh, and I must say the food is amazing, Ma'am, especially the chicken dish."

"I made the chicken," Ke blurted out before she realized it. Throughout the entire dinner while Jax and the elder women conversed, she and Terry sat discreetly across from each other sneakily exchanging flirtatious looks. Although they had never seen or spoken to each other before the funeral, both of them felt a chemistry or a vibe that needed to be explored.

"Well, Mr. T.J., I'm glad you are. I'm glad you are enjoying the chicken." Mecia gave both he and Ke a knowing wink. "If Jax brung you here, especially on a day like this, he must think highly of you, so welcome to the family. "

"Thank you, Ma'am," Terry gave his respects and appreciation.

"Can I ask how it is you know my son, Mr. T.J.?" Mecia asked. "Ya look closer to Marcus' age than Jax's."

"Uhm, well… I uh… I'm an aspiring hip-hop and R&B artist and not long ago, Jax discovered me and has been giving me the opportunity to prove myself and chase my dreams," Terry answered, omitting a few parts on how they actually met.

Before Mecia could dig more out of Terry, Kam cut in. "Oh, so you're the T.J. Stephen won't shut up about in the studio. He keeps sayin' you're gonna be the next big act on Hub City Records." The hint of jealousy Kam displayed was transparent.

"I ain't gonna toot my own horn, but I like to think I am

pretty good at what I do. I believe with the right people behind me, along with my work ethic, I can and will be the next big act," Terry spoke proudly, capitalizing on Kam's jealousy.

"You know what they say, thinking ain't everyone's strong suit," Kam said with a dramatic eye roll. She really wasn't jealous of Terry, she was just giving him a hard time because she caught the looks he gave Ke and she, as well as Jax, was over protective.

"Excuse me, Ma'am, may I use your restroom please?" Terry asked Mecia kindly.

"Of course, second door on the left, just down the hall," Mecia pointed.

"Don't forget to wash your hands," Kam joked but was serious at the same time.

"Oh, Kam, behave yourself and don't be rude to our guest," Mecia scolded.

Terry relieved his bladder, washed his hands and looked himself in the crystal clear mirror. He was up to no good and his next action would prove so.

Quietly, he opened the mirror, revealing fully stocked three-tiered medicine shelves. The orange-clear tubes varied in size and pill quantity. Carefully he inspected the labels in search of the pharmaceutical provider. In no time, he found what he was looking for and replaced the bottles before leaving the restroom.

"You boys gonna stay for dessert?" Mecia asked.

"Not this time, Ma. If you could, just cut us a few slices to go," Jax replied as he rose to meet Terry who was re-entering the dining area.

"Okay, just give me a second," Mecia said and disappeared into the kitchen.

Meanwhile, Jax and Terry said their goodbyes to everyone. Terry said how nice it was to meet everyone and shook their hands, but only Ke's did he caress tenderly.

Mecia returned with two Saran-wrapped slabs of heaven and hugged and kissed Jax's face before they left.

22

CHESS MOVES

TERRY LAID COMFORTABLY on the couch in Lil Vicc's living room, making mental notes of his hard day's work. He found so many angles he could round on his hellish quest for vengeance, but he wanted to make sure he made his moves just right so as not to expose his hand.

Secretly, Terry was playing a real-life game of chess with Jax and was currently a few moves ahead, nearing a smooth checkmate. The match was indeed unorthodox. There were no pawns, only vital power pieces. That meant there was no room for mistakes. Strategy was key!

After an hour of deep thought and calming meditation, Terry knew which way he would attack next. He gathered himself, then reloaded the duffle bag he'd stolen from D. Lee and Greedy with only half the money. He found the key to Lil Vicc's old Lexus and left.

He was a good ten minutes away from Lil Vicc's and almost to his destination when he realized he was driving!

It was actually his first time ever operating a vehicle and surprisingly, he was doing quite well.

Terry had spent so much time in and out of lock up, that he never officially learned how to drive or do other things most kids his age were doing. But so far, so good.

Soon, he exited the uncharacteristically lifeless freeway, following the route he'd seen Jax drive once before. Mimicking his nemesis, Terry pulled into the decent neighborhood tucked away behind the park. He parked across the street from the brick home and watched as a dramatic scene played out right before him.

———

"Well, fuck you then, bitch! I don't need your fat ass no way… Shit, I'm out this muthafucka!" Kenny spat crucially.

"Hmph!" Cori twisted her neck in ghetto fashion. "I sho' wasn't fat when you were beggin' to eat this pussy though, now was I? Bitch ass, broke ass nigga! You ain't got no room to be tryna talk about some damn body," Cori shot back.

Kenny stopped dead in his tracks, retracted a few steps and turned towering over the five-foot nothin' Cori, with a raised fist. "Bitch, you better watch how the fuck you talkin' to me, fo' I fuck around and beat yo' ass out here!" he threatened.

Unmoved, Cori stood her ground. "Nigga, I wish the fuck you would touch me, I'll call my baby daddy!" she warned, using Jax as leverage.

Kenny took a step closer and Cori took one back and pulled out her cell from somewhere in her shirt. They were in a stalemate.

"You ain't even worth my time," Kenny backed down. At the mention of Jax's presence, a bolt of fear passed through Kenny. He knew better than to play those type of games with that man, so he got in his beat-up Cutlass Supreme and left.

———

"Right on time," Terry said to himself as he got out the car. "Here goes nothing."

Cori stood barefoot in her yard and watched as the tail-lights on the Cutlass began to fade down the street. She was bothered but wouldn't show it. It hurt to know she was now single again and just as broke as Kenny. But at least she still had her baby boy, Jr. He'd always be by momma's side. *Always*, she thought.

"Excuse me, Ma'am, are you okay?" Terry appeared before Cori, working his God-given charm and flashing a clean smile.

"Yes, I'm fine. Um, how can I help you?" Cori asked with a blank look.

"Actually, I'm here to help you, Cori."

"Help me how?" Cori eyed the stranger with great suspicion.

"Well, my name is T.J. I'm a friend of Jax's and—"

"Jax? What the fuck does he want? I know damn well you bet not be here to serve me no muthafuckin' papers again, 'cause I ain't goin' to court again!'" Cori spazzed out.

"No, see you got this all wrong. Like I said, I'm here to help you and I'm positive you'll love my kind of help," Terry winked.

"What kind of help are you offering?" Cori asked curiously.

"Well, I was hoping maybe we could have this conversation inside, you know somewhere more private."

"Hell no! My son is inside. And how do I know this ain't some kind of set up or something like that?"

Without hesitation, Terry unzipped the duffle he carried on his shoulder, showing Cori two hundred and fifty thousand reasons why they needed to have that conversation in private.

Once inside her home, Terry revealed to Cori some of his hidden agenda with Jax and the role he needed her to play in order to receive the two hundred and fifty-thousand-dollar payment. It didn't come as a surprise to Terry that Cori was beyond excited to play her part in hurting Jax. The money only made it easier. Go figure.

———

As Terry made it safely back to Lil Vicc's house, he broke out in a thick sweat and his skin began to crawl when he noticed the unmarked police cruiser in the driveway. Spending so much time incarcerated as a youth, he developed a knack for spotting law enforcement personnel and their vehicles a mile away.

Aware of his very recent illegal actions, Terry was overly curious to know what the cop was doing there. He parked curbside and approached the house with extreme caution. Walking around a few shrubs that obscured the pathway to the front door, Terry saw an older white man in a suit, attempting to peer inside a dark window at the front of the house.

"Excuse me, sir, can I help you?" Terry startled the man.

"Ahh," the man fought to suppress his surprise. "Uh-hm, yes, I'm looking for an old associate of mine by the name of Victor Michaels. I've been trying to locate him for at least a week now with no luck. Uh, you may know him by Lil Vicc?" the man said.

Old associate? Terry thought. Instantly, even without a proper introduction he knew exactly who the old, blonde-haired, blue-eyed devil was. It had to be the officer named Sullivan that Lil Vicc mentioned to Jax during his last breaths.

"May I ask what it is you need to speak with my father about that's so important, you came by unannounced?" Terry prodded.

"Father? Wait a sec, I wasn't aware Victor had a kid," Sullivan said. He was baffled.

Terry thought a full second before replying. "Well, I'm not his biological son, but blood couldn't make us any closer. But fuck all that. What's this about, Officer?"

"It's Detective. Detective Sullivan," he corrected. "I was actually coming by to give Victor my thanks in person. See, me and your father go way back. Some info he gave me back in the day elevated me from a lousy traffic cop to a promising young detective. Now, the info he shared recently will put me in a position to become the chief. But I also believe that information he released to me may have put his life in imminent danger. So, I am here to check on his well-being. Please tell me Victor is okay."

The nervous twitch of Terry's left eye and the lowering of his head spoke volumes, without him saying a word! He truly wanted to lie and deceive the detective, but his body reacted faster than his brain.

"Fuck!" Sullivan expressed with a long exhale. "I fucking knew it! Goddammit, I knew he was playing with fire on this one… This shit has BIG D stink all over it!" Sullivan paused for a second, then said, "Can you tell me what happened, kid?"

"There's nothing you can do to help me, Detective. What's done is done. I can handle it from here!" Terry's voice carried frustration.

"Actually, there's a lot I can do to help, kid. See, me and Vicc had a special relationship, you know? A one hand washes the other type deal. By the look in your eyes, I can see his death is eating at you and I refuse to let that asshole BIG D win! Why don't you help carry on your father's legacy and help me bury that sick fuck!" Sullivan's passion was intense. Clearly, his grudge with BIG D was deep-seated.

Something in the detective's proposal lit a proverbial fire under Terry's ass and made him want to help the man. Perhaps it was the mention of Lil Vicc's so-called legacy. He felt like he owed Lil Vicc. Plus, Terry saw the value of including Sullivan into his shiesty fold.

"Why are you so sure BIG D had a hand in this particular situation? Everyone knows he's been locked up for years and if I'm right, you're the one responsible for that, correct?" Terry quizzed.

"I know he's involved because Lil Vicc's partly the reason we were able to arrest him years ago. All the drugs that have been flooding the city in recent years have his signature stamp on them and the operation we busted a few nights ago harbored a massive amount of these same drugs. As you now know, Lil Vicc was the C.I. who gave me the info and whereabouts on the operation. The bust that will lead to my probable promotion was surely the one that cost him his life," Sullivan surmised.

"I see," Terry nodded.

"Now what I want to know is who was behind Vicc's murder, because that will lead me to who is running his operation now. If I can shut it down, it will crush BIG D once and for all. It won't take away an ounce of the pain he's caused me, but any form of payback will do my heart some good."

"Well, Detective, I know exactly who was behind the murder and who is running the show now, because they are one and the same person," Terry revealed. His agenda was beginning to take dangerous form.

The detective's eyes widened and his heart began to race in anticipation of the suspect's name.

Terry continued throwing a devious plan together as he spoke. "I can't give you his name because this man and I have history and it's beyond personal. This situation with him has to be handled by me and me only! As consolation, what I can give you so you can settle your scores with BIG D, is his nephew," Terry informed with an evil grin.

"I'm all ears, kid."

"Are you sure, Detective? I mean, I don't wanna drag you into—"

"Stop jerkin' me around, kid, and give me something!" The detective was indeed anxious.

"Are you into sports, Detective?" Terry asked, setting up the play.

"Always been a huge Texas Tech Red Raider football fan!" Sully said with beaming pride.

"What a coincidence. I take it you are familiar with the name Marcus Cook then, huh?"

"Of course, he's the number two recruit in the country! He's already been labeled as Tech's savior and the kid hasn't even hit the field yet!" Sullivan went into complete fan mode.

"So sad… Now he's simply a target! Marcus is an unwilling participant in a game he doesn't quite know all the rules to," Terry said.

"I'm sorry, I don't seem to follow." Sully scratched his gray-haired head.

"Then let me be very clear, Detective. Marcus Cook is the younger brother to my life-long nemesis and the nephew of your rival, BIG D. But now, thanks to me, Marcus will be seen in the eyes of our community and public as a murderer who recently committed a brutal double homicide. Sir, if you can provide me with a blanket of protection while I carry out the remainder of my well-thought-out plans, then I can provide you with the weapon to make the charges stick on Marcus. You can handle him however you see fit. Trust me, if Lil Vicc's help got you to your position as a detective, fuckin' with me you'll be sitting behind a desk labeled Captain Sullivan soon! So... what do you say? How far are you willing to go for revenge?"

TO BE CONTINUED…
MY BROTHER'S KEEPER 2

AVENGE THY BRETHREN
COMING SOON!

MY BROTHER'S KEEPER 2
AVENGE THY BRETHREN
PREVIEW

"How far am I willing to go for revenge? Kid, in order to repay BIG D for the heinous acts he committed, I will personally break my oath and every law I enforce daily to condemn his soul to the pits of hell, as well as anyone within his bloodline," Detective Sullivan spoke to Terry and meant every word.

"Sounds to me like this BIG D character has cut you deep. Almost as deep as his hoe ass nephew has cut me. What did he do, other than the obvious?" Terry questioned. He knew of BIG D, but didn't know him.

"I'd rather not speak of that evil and get too worked up.

What I would like to know is what other information you can give me on this Marcus Cook guy, and for you to tell me in detail what exactly your plans are for your retribution. "

Terry wasn't big on putting people in his business, especially strangers and law enforcement but he needed Detective Sullivan in his corner. He needed that veil of protection for the shit he was about to do.

By the time Terry finished informing Detective Sullivan on his wicked intentions, the man was completely flabbergasted.

"My God, BIG D was as evil as they come. But you! You are downright sinister! You know what though, this is exactly what we need. I now see the only way to defeat evil is with greater evil. I will handle Marcus and we will let that blow sink in. As soon as the dust settles, you may begin to wreak havoc and exact your wrath. You have my word you will be protected and no legal troubles will come your way, so long as this plan stays between us. I'm going to tell you now though, anyone related or in deep with BIG D is to be considered dangerous, so be careful," Sullivan said before extending his arm for a handshake.

As they shook in agreement, Detective Sullivan said, "By the way, what's your name, kid?"

"In this partnership between me and you, names aren't important, actions are. But for the sake of communication, if need be, you can call me T.J."

"Well, Mr. T.J. , here's my card. Call if you ever need me. Although, it would be best if we actually never spoke again, considering what the future holds."

———

"Okay baby, you be careful now. Behave yourself and remember to call me. Don't be up there at that school actin' a fool. Your ass ain't too old or too big to be beat!" Mecia said to her youngest son Marcus, as they said their goodbyes.

Marcus was finally leaving the nest and on the way to college. She was saddened by his departure, but also proud as a parent should be.

"Don't go off and forget your ol' momma now," she said seriously.

"C'mon, Ma, you know better than that. If it weren't for you I wouldn't even be here, so I could never forget you. I love you. I'll call later and I'll be by to visit at the end of the week," Marcus said sincerely, before leaving his childhood home and heading into adulthood.

Marcus was a good kid who was destined for great things. He had his whole life in front of him. But as we all know, sometimes life is short. From the day we enter this world and take our first breaths, our days are numbered and no one but God really knows when their time will be up.

———

Pure joy and excitement filled Marcus' heart, as he backed out his mother's driveway. As he drove the path to his destination, he couldn't stop smiling ear to ear. In no time, he was within minutes of the enormous campus. Since Marcus grew up in the city, he'd seen the Texas Tech University campus at least a million times, but this time seeing the school was completely different. He felt in his bones he was about to be a part of something great, something special!

Drawing closer to his new home, Marcus decided to celebrate somewhat and listen to one more song before his arrival. He turned up the volume as high as it would go, catching the tail end of one of his favorite songs, "I'm Not Racist" by Joyner Lucas.

"I'm not racist, but I cry a lot/You don't know what its like to be in a frying pot/You don't know what its like to mind your business and get stopped by the cops and not know if you 'bout to die or not/You worry 'bout your life, so you take mine/I love you but I fuckin' hate you at the same time/I wish we could trade shoes or we could change lives/So we could understand each other more but that'll take time/I'm not racist/Its like we livin' in the same building', but splittin' the both sides/I'm not racist/But there's two sides to every story and now you know mine/Can't erase the scars with a bandage/I'm hopin' maybe we can come to an understandin'/Agree to disagree and we can have an understandin'/I"m not racist..."

As the socially conscious song concluded and the beat began to fade from the bass boosted speakers, Marcus' eyes graced the rear view mirror, after hearing a sound most men in this day and age have grown to fear, police sirens!

The next events to follow only heightened the irony of the oh-so-real rap lyrics Marcus was in tune with just seconds prior.

"Shit!" Marcus cursed out loud as he wisely pulled over

into a surprisingly bare IHOP parking lot on the corner of N. University and 19th Street. Immediately, beads of sweat began to trickle down his forehead when his Maserati came to a complete stop and the black Crown Victoria swiftly pulled in right behind him, with the cherry on the roof still flashing.

Marcus was a nervous wreck, still sitting in the driver's seat motionless, with both hands on the wheel. Under the careful watch of Jax all his life, Marcus never even came close to breaking the law. He wasn't speeding. He had a license, insurance and any other requirements needed to operate the vehicle, so he was puzzled as to what could be the reason for the stop.

True enough, Marcus was young and had a lot to learn, but he was not totally naive to the wicked ways of the world. He was well aware of the raging epidemic in America, which was police or any other authority figures killing unarmed black males at an alarming rate, for no reason in most cases. Armed with this public knowledge, Marcus didn't dare to make any sudden moves as he watched the pale officer in dark sunglasses approach the driver's side window, hand planted firmly on the butt of his firearm.

The names Tamir Rice, Mike Brown, Oscar Grant and many more flashed through Marcus' mind. He said a silent prayer in hopes that he would not suffer the same fate as they did, all at the hands of those who swore to protect citizens of this country, no matter their shape, size or color.

"Hello Officer, what seems to be the problem?" Marcus asked nervously.

The man peered down at Marcus with a smirk and said, "Actually, it's Detective… Detective Sullivan," with pride.

"My apologies, Detective. Um, how may I help you? Have I done something wrong?" Marcus questioned, still stiff as a board.

"That's exactly what I'm here to find out, kid. Now tell me, is your name Marcus Cook?" Sullivan asked, already knowing the answer based off the information given by Terry.

"Yes sir, I am Marcus Cook. May I ask what this is all about, Detective?" Marcus spoke cautiously.

"Mr. Cook, are you aware that you have been wanted for questioning in connection to a double homicide for approximately two weeks now?" Sullivan let the lie roll off his tongue fluidly.

Marcus' heart rate quickened and his breaths shortened in awe of the Detective's fictitious statement.

"Sir, there has to be some kind of mistake. I-I'm sure of it. There's no way it could be me you're looking for."

"Well, I'm sure if that's true, we can clear this issue up with no problem and I'll send you on your way. All I need is to run your info through my computer system and we'll know the truth within a matter of minutes. May I see your license and registration, please?" Sullivan asked, as his eyes quickly scanned his surroundings once more. He was about to do the unthinkable.

"Yes sir, no problem," Marcus said respectfully. He was scared as fuck! "I'm going to lift up just a bit and retrieve my wallet from my back pocket now." Marcus did as he said slowly and watched the detective's grip tighten on the deadly weapon, while the man watched him like a hawk. In a snail-like fashion, Marcus retrieved his license and handed it over to the detective through the window.

As if unpleased, Sullivan said, "Registration please," with slight irritation. Marcus felt like something was extremely off, and indeed it was. But he followed the orders given to him.

Sullivan stood a mere foot-and-a-half away from the Maserati door, waiting with grave anticipation for the moment only seconds away. A sliver of reprisal that took almost sixteen years to gain. Sending BIG D away to a cushy federal penitentiary all those years ago did nothing for the misery and emptiness that became of his life without Nancy. In order to remotely feel whole again, Sully wanted an eye-for-an-eye.

In the same slow pace, Marcus reached over and moved to open the glovebox. Pulling the lever, Marcus instantly noticed a difference in the weight of the compartment door but ignored it as the glovebox swung open. He stuck his right hand in blindly and felt the cold steel press against his fingertips. Unknowingly, he'd just placed his fingerprints on the exact automatic weapon that claimed the lives of D. Lee and Greedy B.

Before he had the chance to make sense of the setup occurring in real time, Detective Sullivan withdrew his weapon and opened fire at close range, emptying the clip on his unsuspecting victim in broad daylight.

All seventeen shots fired hit the intended target and pushed Marcus' soul from the earth. As Sullivan's murderous rage subsided, he spoke, "Sorry kid, you were just a means to a very necessary end." He truly wasn't the least bit remorseful for his recent actions. In fact, he felt better already having finally avenged the death of his late wife, whose life was snuffed away at the hands of Marcus' uncle, BIG D, years ago.

After savoring the moment for as long as possible, Sully picked up his phone and called in the situation at hand, using whatever code law enforcement now used for cold blooded murder by cop.

Sullivan's only regret in the matter was now once more Texas Tech's football team was hopeless, all at his selfish hand. But he deemed it a small price to pay. Over the years he'd always told himself he'd do anything for revenge… Anything!

ABOUT THE AUTHOR

Jaquille M. White, is a twenty-nine -year-old African American novelist, who hails from Lubbock, Texas. He is the sole author of the HUB CITY MENACE series and is actively working to pump out new content. Although his books are purely fictional, he writes with such cinematic realism that readers from all walks of life can relate to. Especially those from "Urban" communities who've personally experienced the struggle as he has. He is a loving father, son, brother, uncle, nephew, grandson, cousin, friend and man.

White is incarcerated within the Texas Department of Criminal Justice system, serving out the remainder of a seven-year sentence issued in 2017. Every day he works diligently to better himself in the mind, body and spirit in preparation of his release.

For more on the author, add him on social media or reach out to him personally via US Postal Service or JPAY @ J. White #2226599, 2101 FM 369 N., James V. Allred Unit, Iowa Park, TX, 76367.

Follow on Facebook - @ JWhite Presents
Follow on Instagram - @ JWhitePresents

The Urban Questionnaire

Discussion Questions For The Readers

Questions to help form a full understanding and shape personal opinions.

Prologue - The prologue in *Hub City Menace* is set sometime in the year of 2013 in the ghetto of a fictional Lubbock, Texas hood. Throughout its initial pages, it offers a full back story on the neighborhood itself, as well as its previous occupants. As you've now completed book one, do you see the relevance the author tried to convey and can you piece together the connections all the mentioned characters have with each other in one way or another?

1) The real story begins as Jax finds himself in a predicament he has yet to face. Loss... In your opinion, how well did he handle the situation at hand? Would you have done the same, better or worse?

2) In comparison to chapter one, chapter two lightens in contrast immediately showing the different dimensions to Jax's character. Is his change in demeanor and lack of sympathy for his prior heinous crime realistic in today's world, or simply a quality only urban novels seem to capture?

3) Following Mecia's wishes, Jax goes to visit his uncle Derrick in the feds. Before learning the details of the visit, had you already pieced together uncle Derrick's identity?

Was Derrick's offer to Jax a surprise or did you see it coming?

4) Upon learning that his uncle Derrick is actually one and the same with the legendary BIG D, Jax realizes the seriousness of his mission. Could you immediately guess what the ten bitches were?

5) Now knowing what the ten bitches are and what is to be done with something of such quality, could you accurately guess what lies within the Black Book? Learning who has the Black Book, do you understand why? Hearing bits and pieces about Tina's physical description and her life over the last decade, could you easily figure out the negative role she played in the prologue and what caused friction between her and BIG D long ago?

6) The contents of the infamous Black Book are revealed. Did you expect more or less? How did the revelation of GOAT being BIG D's eyes make you feel knowing how his demise took place and why?

7) When Jax catches Kam at the club, do you feel he was being overprotective? How do you think the situation with CHRISTO was handled? Good or bad move?

8) What's your first impression of Lil Vicc? Does he seem solid? When Jax sensed an ill feeling of Lil Vicc's passenger, what were your thoughts?

9) When Les is introduced at the pharmacy, what was your first impression? Could you guess the underlying tension between her and her stepdaughter Tory and what may have caused it?

10) Greedy B. and D. Lee appear in chapter ten for the first time. Outside of being best friends for years, what drives their loyalty to Jax?

11) Did you enjoy BIG D's sense of humor when he's playing with Jax about fuckin' Tina? Did ya understand the strategic move he made? Did the revelation of CHRISTO actually being the plug surprise you?

12) Was Jax's move on a "Front" cliché to you or quite fitting, given the scenario?

13) Jax's mind is set on building the studio and starting a legit label. What would you have done instead?

14) As we skip six years ahead, did you expect for Hub City Records to grow as exponentially as it did and enjoy the throes of mainstream success? Everyone's life seemed to be lovely and somewhat perfect. Was this also an expectation?

15) The second Tuck called "collect" what was your first thought of what happened? How far off were you? Who did you peg as the anonymous caller and why? What's your first impression of the guard Angela and her devotion to BIG D?

16) When Lil Vicc is outlined as the snitch, how did you expect his impending demise? What are your thoughts of Juan and Jose? How do you feel of Lil Vicc and Terry's relationship? How would you react if you were in Terry's shoes and you witnessed the murderer of your brother murder your father figure as well?

17) If you were Terry, would you strategize to kill Jax, or simply do it at first opportunity? Can you picture Roxy? What are your thoughts of her? What did you think when she and Terry have a chance encounter? Was Terry's plan as good as he thought or dangerously crazy knowing Jax's power?

18) Did Terry infiltrate Jax's circle easier than you thought? What's your take on his studio performance? How do you feel about Hot Boi? When Cori summons Jax over, did you expect him to handle her like that? Was he in the right or wrong?

19) Did you expect more of an epic gun battle when Terry kills D. Lee and Greedy? Did their death invoke any emotions in you, if so what? Can you pinpoint the comedy in Fudda Mayne's and Deezy's argument prior to discovering D. Lee and Greedy? Did you piece together who Deezy's real baby daddy is? How was Terry's performance showing up moments after Jax finds his slain comrades?

20) Is Jax naive for immediately taking to Terry? Would you not have? Was it that hard to see through his facade?

21) Terry's hatred for Jax is clear, but is it justified? Was he wrong for involving Jax's loved ones in his twisted game of revenge? What do you think of Ke's and Terry's obvious crush at first sight? What do you think of Kam's rudeness to Terry, was it more so of musical jealousy of her being protective of Ke?

22) What did you think Terry was initially going to do when he approached Cori? Did you think she'd roll on Jax so easily? When Terry and the detective link up conspiring on Marcus, what's your guess of his fate?

Extra Questions

1) So far in book one, who is your favorite character and why?

2) What's your favorite chapter and why?

3) Are you in favor of the protagonist or antagonist?

4) On a scale of 1 – 10, how do you rate book one?

LOCK DOWN PUBLICATIONS AND CA$H PRESENTS

ASSISTED PUBLISHING PACKAGES

BASIC PACKAGE

$499

Editing

Cover Design

Formatting

UPGRADED PACKAGE

$800

Typing

Editing

Cover Design

Formatting

ADVANCE PACKAGE

$1,200

Typing

Editing

Cover Design

Formatting

Copyright registration

Proofreading

Upload book to Amazon

LDP SUPREME PACKAGE

$1,500

Typing

Editing

Cover Design

Formatting

Copyright registration

Proofreading

Set up Amazon account

Upload book to Amazon

Advertise on LDP, Amazon and Facebook Page

Submission Guidelines

Submit the first three chapters of your completed manuscript to ldpsubmissions@gmail.com. In the subject line add Your Book's Title. The manuscript must be in a Word Doc file and sent as an attachment. Document should be in Times New Roman, double spaced, and in size 12 font. Also, provide your synopsis and full contact information. If sending multiple submissions, they must each be in a separate email.

Have a story but no way to send it electronically? You can still submit to LDP/Ca$h Presents. Send in the first three chapters, written or typed, of your completed manuscript to:

LDP: Submissions Dept
P.O. Box 944
Stockbridge, GA 30281-9998

DO NOT send original manuscript. Must be a duplicate.
Provide your synopsis and a cover letter containing your full contact information.

Thanks for considering LDP and Ca$h Presents.

NEW RELEASES

BLOODLINE OF A SAVAGE 1&2
THESE VICIOUS STREETS 1&2
RELENTLESS GOON
RELENTLESS GOON 2
BY PRINCE A. TAUHID

THE BUTTERFLY MAFIA 1-3
BY FUMIYA PAYNE

A THUG'S STREET PRINCESS 1&2
BY MEESHA

CITY OF SMOKE 2
BY MOLOTTI

STEPPERS 1,2&3
THE REAL BADDIES OF CHI-RAQ
BY KING RIO

THE LANE 1&2
BY KEN-KEN SPENCE

THUG OF SPADES 1&2
LOVE IN THE TRENCHES 2
CORNER BOYS
BY COREY ROBINSON

TIL DEATH 3

BY ARYANNA

THE BIRTH OF A GANGSTER 4
BY DELMONT PLAYER

PRODUCT OF THE STREETS 1&2
BY DEMOND "MONEY" ANDERSON

NO TIME FOR ERROR
BY KEESE

MONEY HUNGRY DEMONS
BY TRANAY ADAMS

STANDING ON HER BUSINESS 2
BY DG SANTANA

TENDER
BY KHUFU

HUB CITY MENACE
BY JAQUILLE M. WHITE

Coming Soon from Lock Down Publications/Ca$h Presents

IF YOU CROSS ME ONCE 6
ANGEL V
By Anthony Fields

IMMA DIE BOUT MINE 5
By Aryanna

A THUGS STREET PRINCESS 3
By Meesha

PRODUCT OF THE STREETS 3
By Demond Money Anderson

CORNER BOYS 2
By Corey Robinson

THE MURDER QUEENS 6&7
By Michael Gallon

CITY OF SMOKE 3
By Molotti

CONFESSIONS OF A DOPE BOY
By Nicholas Lock

THA TAKEOVER
By Keith Chandler

BETRAYAL OF A G 2
By Ray Vinci

CRIME BOSS
By Playa Ray

Available Now

RESTRAINING ORDER 1 & 2
By CA$H & Coffee

LOVE KNOWS NO BOUNDARIES 1-3
By Coffee

RAISED AS A GOON I, II, III & IV
BRED BY THE SLUMS I, II, III
BLAST FOR ME I & II
ROTTEN TO THE CORE I II III
A BRONX TALE I, II, III
DUFFLE BAG CARTEL I II III IV V VI
HEARTLESS GOON I II III IV V
A SAVAGE DOPEBOY I II
DRUG LORDS I II III
CUTTHROAT MAFIA I II
KING OF THE TRENCHES
By Ghost

LAY IT DOWN I & II
LAST OF A DYING BREED I II
BLOOD STAINS OF A SHOTTA I & II III
By Jamaica

LOYAL TO THE GAME I II III
LIFE OF SIN I, II III
By TJ & Jelissa

IF LOVING HIM IS WRONG…I & II
LOVE ME EVEN WHEN IT HURTS I II III
By Jelissa

PUSH IT TO THE LIMIT
By Bre' Hayes

BLOODY COMMAS I & II
SKI MASK CARTEL I, II & III
KING OF NEW YORK I II, III IV V
RISE TO POWER I II III
COKE KINGS I II III IV V
BORN HEARTLESS I II III IV
KING OF THE TRAP I II
By T.J. Edwards

WHEN THE STREETS CLAP BACK I & II III
THE HEART OF A SAVAGE I II III IV
MONEY MAFIA I II
LOYAL TO THE SOIL I II III
By Jibril Williams

A DISTINGUISHED THUG STOLE MY HEART I
II & III
LOVE SHOULDN'T HURT I II III IV
RENEGADE BOYS 1-4
PAID IN KARMA 1-3

SAVAGE STORMS 1-3
AN UNFORESEEN LOVE 1-3
BABY, I'M WINTERTIME COLD 1-3
A THUG'S STREET PRINCESS 1&2
By Meesha

A GANGSTER'S CODE 1-3
A GANGSTER'S SYN 1-3
THE SAVAGE LIFE 1-3
CHAINED TO THE STREETS 1-3
BLOOD ON THE MONEY 1-3
A GANGSTA'S PAIN 1-3
BEAUTIFUL LIES AND UGLY TRUTHS
CHURCH IN THESE STREETS
By J-Blunt

CUM FOR ME 1-8
An LDP Erotica Collaboration

BLOOD OF A BOSS 1-5
SHADOWS OF THE GAME
TRAP BASTARD
By Askari

THE STREETS BLEED MURDER 1-3
THE HEART OF A GANGSTA 1-3
By Jerry Jackson

WHEN A GOOD GIRL GOES BAD
By Adrienne

THE COST OF LOYALTY 1-3
By Kweli

BRIDE OF A HUSTLA 1-3
THE FETTI GIRLS 1-3
CORRUPTED BY A GANGSTA 1-4
BLINDED BY HIS LOVE
THE PRICE YOU PAY FOR LOVE 1-3
DOPE GIRL MAGIC 1-3
By Destiny Skai

A KINGPIN'S AMBITION
A KINGPIN'S AMBITION II
I MURDER FOR THE DOUGH
By Ambitious

TRUE SAVAGE 1-7
DOPE BOY MAGIC 1-3
MIDNIGHT CARTEL 1-3
CITY OF KINGZ 1&2
NIGHTMARE ON SILENT AVE
THE PLUG OF LIL MEXICO 1&2
CLASSIC CITY
By Chris Green

A GANGSTER'S REVENGE 1-4
THE BOSS MAN'S DAUGHTERS 1-5
A SAVAGE LOVE 1&2
BAE BELONGS TO ME 1&2
A HUSTLER'S DECEIT 1-3
WHAT BAD BITCHES DO 1-3

SOUL OF A MONSTER 1-3
KILL ZONE
A DOPE BOY'S QUEEN 1-3
TIL DEATH 1-3
IMMA DIE BOUT MINE 1-4
By Aryanna

A DOPEBOY'S PRAYER
By Eddie "Wolf" Lee

THE KING CARTEL 1-3
By Frank Gresham

THESE NIGGAS AIN'T LOYAL 1-3
By Nikki Tee

GANGSTA SHYT 1-3
By CATO

THE ULTIMATE BETRAYAL
By Phoenix

BOSS'N UP 1-3
By Royal Nicole

I LOVE YOU TO DEATH
By Destiny J

I RIDE FOR MY HITTA
I STILL RIDE FOR MY HITTA
By Misty Holt

LOVE & CHASIN' PAPER
By Qay Crockett

TO DIE IN VAIN
SINS OF A HUSTLA
By ASAD

BROOKLYN HUSTLAZ
By Boogsy Morina

BROOKLYN ON LOCK 1 & 2
By Sonovia

GANGSTA CITY
By Teddy Duke

A DRUG KING AND HIS DIAMOND 1-3
A DOPEMAN'S RICHES
HER MAN, MINE'S TOO 1&2
CASH MONEY HO'S
THE WIFEY I USED TO BE 1&2
PRETTY GIRLS DO NASTY THINGS
By Nicole Goosby

LIPSTICK KILLAH 1-3
CRIME OF PASSION 1-3
FRIEND OR FOE 1-3
By Mimi

TRAPHOUSE KING 1-3
KINGPIN KILLAZ 1-3

STREET KINGS 1&2
PAID IN BLOOD 1&2
CARTEL KILLAZ 1-3
DOPE GODS 1&2
By Hood Rich

THE STREETS ARE CALLING
By Duquie Wilson

STEADY MOBBN' 1-3
THE STREETS STAINED MY SOUL 1-3
By Marcellus Allen

WHO SHOT YA 1-3
SON OF A DOPE FIEND 1-4
HEAVEN GOT A GHETTO 1&2
SKI MASK MONEY 1&2
By Renta

GORILLAZ IN THE BAY 1-4
TEARS OF A GANGSTA 1/&2
3X KRAZY 1&2
STRAIGHT BEAST MODE 1&2
By DE'KARI

TRIGGADALE 1-3
MURDA WAS THE CASE 1-3
By Elijah R. Freeman

SLAUGHTER GANG 1-3
RUTHLESS HEART 1-3

By Willie Slaughter

GOD BLESS THE TRAPPERS 1-3
THESE SCANDALOUS STREETS 1-3
FEAR MY GANGSTA 1-5
THESE STREETS DON'T LOVE NOBODY 1-2
BURY ME A G 1-5
A GANGSTA'S EMPIRE 1-4
THE DOPEMAN'S BODYGAURD 1&2
THE REALEST KILLAZ 1-3
THE LAST OF THE OGS 1-3
By Tranay Adams

MARRIED TO A BOSS 1-3
By Destiny Skai & Chris Green

KINGZ OF THE GAME 1-7
CRIME BOSS 1-3
By Playa Ray

FUK SHYT
By Blakk Diamond

DON'T F#CK WITH MY HEART 1&2
By Linnea

ADDICTED TO THE DRAMA 1-3
IN THE ARM OF HIS BOSS
By Jamila

LOYALTY AIN'T PROMISED 1&2

By Keith Williams

YAYO 1-4
A SHOOTER'S AMBITION 1&2
BRED IN THE GAME
By S. Allen

TRAP GOD 1-3
RICH $AVAGE 1-3
MONEY IN THE GRAVE 1-3
CARTEL MONEY
By Martell Troublesome Bolden

FOREVER GANGSTA 1&2
GLOCKS ON SATIN SHEETS 1&2
By Adrian Dulan

TOE TAGZ 1-4
LEVELS TO THIS SHYT 1&2
IT'S JUST ME AND YOU
By Ah'Million

KINGPIN DREAMS 1-3
RAN OFF ON DA PLUG
By Paper Boi Rari

THE STREETS MADE ME 1-3
By Larry D. Wright

CONFESSIONS OF A GANGSTA 1-4
CONFESSIONS OF A JACKBOY 1-3

CONFESSIONS OF A HITMAN
By Nicholas Lock

I'M NOTHING WITHOUT HIS LOVE
SINS OF A THUG
TO THE THUG I LOVED BEFORE
A GANGSTA SAVED XMAS
IN A HUSTLER I TRUST
By Monet Dragun

QUIET MONEY 1-3
THUG LIFE 1-3
EXTENDED CLIP 1&2
A GANGSTA'S PARADISE
By Trai'Quan

CAUGHT UP IN THE LIFE 1-3
THE STREETS NEVER LET GO 1-3
By Robert Baptiste

NEW TO THE GAME 1-3
MONEY, MURDER & MEMORIES 1-3
By Malik D. Rice

CREAM 2-3
THE STREETS WILL TALK
By Yolanda Moore

THE STREETS WILL NEVER CLOSE 1-3
By K'ajji

LIFE OF A SAVAGE 1-4
A GANGSTA'S QUR'AN 1-4
MURDA SEASON 1-3
GANGLAND CARTEL 1-3
CHI'RAQ GANGSTAS 1-4
KILLERS ON ELM STREET 1-3
JACK BOYZ N DA BRONX 1-3
A DOPEBOY'S DREAM 1-3
JACK BOYS VS DOPE BOYS 1-3
COKE GIRLZ
COKE BOYS
SOSA GANG 1&2
BRONX SAVAGES
BODYMORE KINGPINS
BLOOD OF A GOON
By Romell Tukes

CONCRETE KILLA 1-3
VICIOUS LOYALTY 1-3
By Kingpen

THE ULTIMATE SACRIFICE 1-6
KHADIFI
IF YOU CROSS ME ONCE 1-3
ANGEL 1-4
IN THE BLINK OF AN EYE
By Anthony Fields

THE LIFE OF A HOOD STAR
By Ca$h & Rashia Wilson

NIGHTMARES OF A HUSTLA 1-3
BLOOD AND GAMES 1&2
By King Dream

GHOST MOB
By Stilloan Robinson

HARD AND RUTHLESS 1&2
MOB TOWN 251
THE BILLIONAIRE BENTLEYS 1-3
REAL G'S MOVE IN SILENCE
By Von Diesel

MOB TIES 1-7
SOUL OF A HUSTLER, HEART OF A KILLER 1-3
GORILLAZ IN THE TRENCHES
By SayNoMore

BODYMORE MURDERLAND 1-3
THE BIRTH OF A GANGSTER 1-4
By Delmont Player

FOR THE LOVE OF A BOSS 1&2
By C. D. Blue

KILLA KOUNTY 1-5
By Khufu

MOBBED UP 1-4
THE BRICK MAN 1-5
THE COCAINE PRINCESS 1-10

STEPPERS 1-3
SUPER GREMLIN 1-4
By King Rio

MONEY GAME 1&2
By Smoove Dolla

A GANGSTA'S KARMA 1-4
By FLAME

KING OF THE TRENCHES 1-3
By GHOST & TRANAY ADAMS

QUEEN OF THE ZOO 1&2
By Black Migo

GRIMEY WAYS 1-3
BETRAYAL OF A G
By Ray Vinci

XMAS WITH AN ATL SHOOTER
By Ca$h & Destiny Skai

KING KILLA 1&2
By Vincent "Vitto" Holloway

BETRAYAL OF A THUG 1&2
By Fre$h

THE MURDER QUEENS 1-5
By Michael Gallon

FOR THE LOVE OF BLOOD 1-4
By Jamel Mitchell

HOOD CONSIGLIERE 1&2
NO TIME FOR ERROR
By Keese

PROTÉGÉ OF A LEGEND 1&2
LOVE IN THE TRENCHES 1&2
By Corey Robinson

THE PLUG'S RUTHLESS DAUGHTER
By Tony Daniels

BORN IN THE GRAVE 1-3
CRIME PAYS
By Self Made Tay

MOAN IN MY MOUTH
By XTASY

TORN BETWEEN A GANGSTER AND A
GENTLEMAN
By J-BLUNT & Miss Kim

LOYALTY IS EVERYTHING 1-3
CITY OF SMOKE 1&2
By Molotti

HERE TODAY GONE TOMORROW 1&2
By Fly Rock

WOMEN LIE MEN LIE 1-4
FIFTY SHADES OF SNOW 1-3
STACK BEFORE YOU SPLURGE
GIRLS FALL LIKE DOMINOES
NAÏVE TO THE STREETS
By ROY MILLIGAN

PILLOW PRINCESS
By S. Hawkins

THE BUTTERFLY MAFIA 1-3
SALUTE MY SAVAGERY 1&2
By Fumiya Payne

THE LANE 1&2
By Ken-Ken Spence

THE PUSSY TRAP 1-5
By Nene Capri

DIRTY DNA
By Blaque

SANCTIFIED AND HORNY
by XTASY

BOOKS BY LDP'S CEO, CA$H

TRUST IN NO MAN

TRUST IN NO MAN 2

TRUST IN NO MAN 3

BONDED BY BLOOD

SHORTY GOT A THUG

THUGS CRY

THUGS CRY 2

THUGS CRY 3

TRUST NO BITCH

TRUST NO BITCH 2

TRUST NO BITCH 3

TIL MY CASKET DROPS

RESTRAINING ORDER

RESTRAINING ORDER 2

IN LOVE WITH A CONVICT

LIFE OF A HOOD STAR

XMAS WITH AN ATL SHOOTER

www.ingramcontent.com/pod-product-compliance
Lightning Source LLC
Chambersburg PA
CBHW071136260626
47162CB00003B/803